Kate's tongue slipped out to moisten her lips and Travis's body reacted immediately.

After holding her close for those long moments, he was so in tune with her, so filled with the sight and scent and feel of her. Now the sight of her tongue stirred him and made him long to taste it and the inside of her mouth. To kiss her and feel her kissing him back, as they'd done back in college, when they were still in love.

But this wasn't the time. Hell, it might never be the right time for that again. This was about Kate and her son, and his attempts to help her get her little boy back. It wasn't about anything else. Certainly nothing to do with him.

"Travis," she said softly, her eyes glittering with dampness.

"I know," he said. "I'm here. I'll be here as long as you need me."

MALLORY KANE

SPECIAL FORCES FATHER

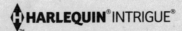

To my family, who always supports me.

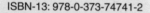

Recycling programs
for this product may
not exist in your area.

ISBN-13: 978-0-373-74741-2

SPECIAL FORCES FATHER

Copyright © 2013 by Rickey R. Mallory

All rights reserved. Except for use in any review, the reproduction or
utilization of this work in whole or in part in any form by any electronic,
mechanical or other means, now known or hereafter invented, including
xerography, photocopying and recording, or in any information storage
or retrieval system, is forbidden without the written permission of the
publisher, Harlequin Enterprises Limited, 225 Duncan Mill Road,
Don Mills, Ontario M3B 3K9, Canada.

This is a work of fiction. Names, characters, places and incidents are
either the product of the author's imagination or are used fictitiously,
and any resemblance to actual persons, living or dead, business
establishments, events or locales is entirely coincidental.

This edition published by arrangement with Harlequin Books S.A.

For questions and comments about the quality of this book,
please contact us at CustomerService@Harlequin.com.

® and TM are trademarks of Harlequin Enterprises Limited or its
corporate affiliates. Trademarks indicated with ® are registered in the
United States Patent and Trademark Office, the Canadian Trade Marks
Office and in other countries.

Printed in U.S.A.

HARLEQUIN®
www.Harlequin.com

ABOUT THE AUTHOR

Mallory Kane has two very good reasons for loving reading and writing. Her mother was a librarian, who taught her to love and respect books as a precious resource. Her father could hold listeners spellbound for hours with his stories. He was always her biggest fan.

She loves romantic suspense with dangerous heroes and dauntless heroines, and enjoys tossing in a bit of her medical knowledge for an extra dose of intrigue. After twenty-five books published, Mallory is still amazed and thrilled that she actually gets to make up stories for a living.

Mallory lives in Tennessee with her computer-genius husband and three exceptionally intelligent cats. She enjoys hearing from readers. You can write her at mallory@mallorykane.com or via Harlequin Books.

Books by Mallory Kane

CAST OF CHARACTERS

Travis Delancey—The army Special Forces operative returns to New Orleans after five months in captivity to reconnect with the woman he has never forgotten. He discovers he has a four-year-old son. Furthermore, his child has been kidnapped, and all his specialized training may not be enough to save him.

Kate Chalmet—This psychiatrist is devastated by the kidnapping of her son, Max. When Travis, his father, shows up at her door, she's torn between her still-burning love for him and her need to protect her son from the man who has a bad habit of leaving.

Myron Stamps—This senior senator is facing trial for assault with a deadly weapon. But someone is so determined to see him acquitted that they've kidnapped Dr. Kate Chalmet's son to force her to find that at the time of the shooting he was temporarily insane.

Darby Sills—Senator Sills is an elder statesman in Louisiana, alongside Myron Stamps. He and Stamps and Gavin Whitley are the last of a group of good old boys who are highly influential in the Louisiana legislature. Sills has the money to hire a kidnapper. Did he?

Gavin Whitley—The congressman is the junior member of Myron Stamps's good old boy's club. Did Stamps and Sills lean on him to hire the kidnapper to make sure Stamps doesn't go to prison?

Bentley Woods—This kidnapper-for-hire was imported from Chicago to abduct Max Chalmet. He's good at his job, but he's also a hired gun. When he finds out the boy's father is a Delancey, he sees a chance to make even more money.

Dawson Delancey—Travis's cousin is a private investigator. He rallies the Delancey boys to help Travis rescue his son.

Chapter One

Travis Delancey knew exactly what Wild Will Hancock was thinking as he eyed Travis's trembling hands. *Drugs.*

That wasn't Travis's problem, but he didn't bother explaining. He just shifted in the creaky wooden chair in the double-wide that served as Wild Will's office and extracted the credit card from the side pocket of his military issue duffel bag. He held it up.

The shiny platinum of the card reflected in Wild Will's pupils.

"Did I mention I'm in a hurry?" Travis asked evenly.

"Yes, sir, you did," Wild Will said, his eyes still glued to the card. "Now, as far as the amount of the down payment—?"

"All of it," Travis broke in.

"All of it." Wild Will's prominent Adam's apple bobbed as he swallowed. "Well then, if you'll just swipe your card right there—" he nodded toward the credit card machine "—I'll get you on your way."

Travis swiped and Wild Will typed. After a torturously slow two minutes of hunting and pecking, the man finally paused, his index fingers poised over the keyboard. "Your current address?"

Travis started to give him his parents' address, then changed his mind. He gave him Kate's address instead. That's where he was headed, and he didn't want anyone calling his parents until he was ready to talk to them himself.

"And driver's license?"

Just as Travis opened his mouth to recite his Louisiana driver's license number, somebody banged loudly on the trailer's metal door. Travis jumped. He instantly recovered and smiled sheepishly, but Wild Will's attention was on the door. "Come in," Will yelled.

The door creaked open to reveal a pudgy man in a T-shirt and jeans.

"Yeah," he said. "I want to drive that Camaro."

Will nodded. "Gimme a minute."

The pudgy guy nodded back. "No prob," he said. He went outside and closed the door.

Will turned back to Travis. "Now, where were we?"

"Driver's license number," Travis answered. He rattled off his and a random future expiration date. His license had actually expired two years before. Army Special Forces officers didn't need civilian driver's licenses, especially while on supersecret missions to unnamed countries overseas.

To his relief, the gaunt man who looked more like an undertaker than a used-car dealer didn't ask to see the license. He merely gestured toward the credit card machine.

Travis scribbled his signature on the screen. His writing was worse than usual because of his trembling hand, but it satisfied Wild Will. It took a few more minutes to finish the paperwork and transfer the title.

"Congratulations. I know you'll enjoy driving this little beauty," Will said.

"Thanks," Travis answered, irony tingeing his voice. The *little beauty* was a ten-year-old domestic hatchback. The tires were relatively new but there was a definite smear of oily smoke on the tailpipe. Still, with any luck, a couple quarts of oil would get him to New Orleans, Louisiana.

After tossing his duffel bag into the back of the car, he jumped in and drove off the lot and onto the interstate. It was over a thousand miles from Bethesda, Maryland, to New Orleans.

Travis squeezed the steering wheel with both hands, then let go with his right hand and inspected it. Still shaking.

Not surprising. He hadn't had any exercise or decent food for five months, unless he counted the protein shakes and flavored gelatin he'd been receiving at Walter Reed National Military Medical Center for the past two weeks. Walking up and down the halls of the psych unit hardly qualified as exercise.

Dr. Gingosian wouldn't be happy that he'd left against medical advice, but Travis wasn't interested in spending even one more day listening to the doctor drone on about post-traumatic stress disorder and other *understandable emotional effects of captivity.*

He knew what was wrong with him and it wasn't PTSD. He'd kept himself sane for five months in the windowless, unheated room where he'd been held by doing three things. Cultivating his hatred of his captors, playing videos of his most treasured memories inside his head and exercising—until lack of nutrition and loss of weight had made him too weak to stand.

He'd learned a lot about himself during that awful time as he had ignored external discomforts and nurtured his memories. When he was brought to Walter Reed, he'd gratefully accepted medical treatment, but he'd quickly figured out that his emotional problems wouldn't be cured by medication or group therapy.

He knew what he needed. He needed the people he loved. His brothers and sister. His mom. Even his dad. At some point, in that dark stinking room where his only means of escape was inside his head, he'd forgiven Robert Delancey for the drunken rages that had been his and his siblings' relationship with their father throughout most of his life.

But the one person he needed the most was Kate. Not that he deserved her. He'd walked out on her twice. The first time he'd stomped out in a fit of anger that had matched the worst his dad could dish out. He'd marched straight from her dorm room to the army recruitment office and enlisted on the spot. The second time, when he'd called her during a rare furlough prior to being shipped overseas, she'd kicked him out. Not in anger, that wasn't Kate's style. No. She'd calmly explained that a one-night stand every few years when he happened to be in town was not her idea of a relationship. She'd told him not to call her again. And he hadn't.

During those horrific five months in captivity, as the rivers of his memories had flowed over him, providing rare and precious moments away from the hunger, cold, filth and torture, he'd discovered that his most treasured memories were of her. And he'd realized that not fighting for her love that last time he'd seen her had been the biggest mistake of his life.

No matter where she was now or who she was with, he needed to find her and apologize for walking out. But he needed something else, too. He needed to look into her eyes and see if the love that had once shone in them for him had really died, or if there was still a spark of it left.

He didn't hold out much hope for a spark. Things had not gone well on that last trip. Okay, *some* things had not gone well. Other things had gone exceptionally well. He'd come home on leave for the first time in two years and called her to see if he could buy her dinner or something. She'd agreed.

The dinner at Commander's Palace had been excellent. The *or something* had been mind-blowing.

By contrast, the next morning had turned out awkward and sad. When Travis had stood at her door telling her he'd call her whenever he could, she'd waved a hand.

"Don't bother," she'd said in her direct, no-nonsense way. "A drop-in every couple years is not my style."

Her words echoed in his head now as he gripped the wheel more tightly and eased the accelerator forward until the little car was doing seventy. He glanced at the clock on the dashboard. Eight o'clock in the evening. Even with bathroom stops and a few hours' sleep at an interstate hotel, he ought to be in New Orleans within twenty-four hours.

What would he say when he saw Kate? A better question might be what was she going to say when he showed up on her doorstep?

THE NEXT MORNING, Dr. Kate Chalmet picked up Myron Stamps's police file. She'd been appointed by the Orleans Parish District Attorney's office to evaluate Senator Stamps, who was pleading temporary insanity in the aggravated assault of Paul Guillame, his former political adviser. She'd cleared her calendar so she could prepare, since the trial was scheduled to begin in ten days.

Kate knew that the senator had shot Paul Guillame during a shoot-out at Paul's house. "Shoot-out," she muttered, shaking her head. Sounded more like a John Wayne movie than an incident in the Lower Garden District in New Orleans. But that's exactly how the police had described it.

She opened the file and glanced over the initial report, which was filed by the first officer on the scene, Halan Matson. She skimmed it.

Upon entering at 4330 Tchoupitoulas Avenue, we observed the exchange of gunfire between four apparent occupants taking cover in the kitchen area of the house and two armed men in the dining room. At that time, we observed that at least one of the occupants was armed.

We entered and arrested the two armed men, both of whom had suffered superficial gunshot wounds. At that point Detective Lucas Delancey arrived and took charge of the scene.

The name Delancey stopped her. Pressing her lips together, she took a deep breath and told herself to see it as Smith or Jones or Rumpelstiltskin—anything but Delancey.

The report described the two gunmen being checked out by EMTs, then taken into custody and Harte Delancey and Paul Guillame, two of the occupants, being transported to local hospitals.

Harte Delancey. Lucas Delancey. The case was awash with Delanceys. She gritted her teeth. *Jones. Smith. Stiltskin.* The names of the people involved had nothing to do with her or why she was reviewing the case.

She glanced through the other reports until she came to the statements given by Harte

Delancey and Danielle Canto. She'd read one paragraph of Canto's statement when her cell phone rang.

"This is Dr. Chalmet," she said.

She heard nothing for a couple seconds. Then a voice spoke in a guttural whisper. "*Dr. Chalmet. You understand that Myron Stamps was insane when he shot that guy, right?*"

Kate was surprised. This wasn't the first time she'd received an anonymous call about a case. It wasn't even the first time she'd been threatened. Although if this was a threat, it was starting off very mildly. Usually the calls came during the trial, once her name was on the witness list, not days ahead of time. Sighing audibly, she asked, "Who is this?"

There was no answer.

"I do not respond to empty anonymous threats," she said archly.

A hollow click told her the person had hung up. She set her phone down and tapped a fingernail on Stamps's file. Who knew she'd been appointed to evaluate the senator? She ticked them off on her fingers. Vinson Akers's secretary, who had called her two weeks ago with the District Attorney's request. Akers himself, of course, and his prosecutors, Melissa Shallowford and Harte Delancey.

Stamps's attorney knew, too, and that meant

there was probably a 99 percent chance that Stamps knew. That probably explained the phone call. The caller might be a supporter, a family member, even a constituent who really thought the senator might be insane. She'd learned a long time ago that harassing, complaining, even threatening calls like this were part of the package if she was going to be a consultant and expert witness for the D.A.'s office. Moreover, she knew it was a waste of time to wonder about the caller's motivation.

She went back to reading Danielle Canto's statement. She'd studied most of the lengthy narrative by lunchtime when her secretary, Alice Stott, stuck her head in.

"Kate, it's eleven-thirty. We need expanding files, pens and a few other things. Want me to go by the office-supply store on my lunch break?"

"Would you rather leave early and pick up the supplies on your way home?" Kate asked. "I'm probably going to leave a little early myself since I don't have any appointments."

Alice smiled. "Leave early? Twist my arm. I'll just run out and grab some lunch. Can I bring you something?"

"I've got yogurt and an apple. I'm fixing Max *pasketti* tonight. We're going to watch *Shrek*."

"Max hasn't seen *Shrek?*" Alice asked.

Kate laughed. "Please," she said. "It hasn't been that long since your kids were little. Of course he has. He's seen all of them. This will be the third time. I just have to convince him that we can only watch one tonight."

Alice chuckled. "I do remember. I'll be back soon."

"Take your time," Kate said, her attention already back on Danielle Canto's statement. She'd finished it and was flipping back through, expanding on the notes she'd taken, when someone rapped on her door facing.

She looked up and for a split second, her lungs seized, and she couldn't get a breath. Then she blinked and realized that the tall lanky man standing in the doorway wasn't Travis Delancey. It was Harte, Travis's younger brother and a prosecutor in the D.A.'s office.

"Hi, Dr. Chalmet," the young man said, smiling. "Your secretary must be at lunch." He held a manila envelope in his right hand. His left arm was in a sling, a result of being shot during that same violent night she'd just been reading about. Harte had undergone surgery to remove a bullet that had lodged alarmingly close to his heart.

She cleared her throat, pushing away the thoughts of how very like Travis he looked. "Mr. Delancey. What can I do for you?"

"Senator Stamps's attorney sent this to the D.A.'s office." He handed her the envelope, which was too thin to hold more than a couple sheets of paper.

"Oh? Did she say what it was?" Kate grabbed a letter opener and slit the seal.

"Apparently it's a report from an independent physician who evaluated Stamps."

Kate glanced at the two sheets of paper. "An independent physician. Hmm."

Harte laughed. "Spoken like a doctor."

Kate glanced up, a little startled by his laugh. The laugh sounded just like Travis, too. She shook her head mentally as she set the envelope on her desk. "Thanks," she said, then nodded toward the sling. "How are you doing?"

Harte shrugged, then winced. "Fine. I'm still sore, but I've been in physical therapy for four weeks now. I'm doing lots better."

She nodded. "I'm glad," she said. "How did you get demoted to courier service? No prosecutor jobs?"

"I'm not supposed to be working, and they're sure not letting me do anything on the Stamps case except be a witness. I'm not even a reliable witness, since I was losing blood the whole time." He looked ruefully at the sling. "At least delivering envelopes gives me a chance to get out and get some exercise, if walking fairly slow can be considered exercise."

Kate smiled. "Well, I appreciate you bringing this over." She paused, then spoke again. "Do you have a few minutes to talk to me about what happened that day?"

"Sure," Harte said. "What do you want to know?"

"I've been through Ms. Canto's statement. I haven't started yours yet. I hadn't decided for sure whether I need to interview you or Ms. Canto, but since you're here, would you mind telling me what you remember about Senator Stamps that day? His demeanor, his level of concentration, was he afraid, angry, acting confused?" She waved a hand. "Things like that."

Harte shifted on his feet and adjusted the sling.

"Please, sit down if that's more comfortable for you."

"Thanks," he said and lowered his lean frame into a chair. "You know, I wasn't kidding when I said I wasn't a very reliable witness. I can tell you what I saw and heard, but when I get on the stand, defense counsel will rip into me like a vulture."

"Because you were wounded?"

Harte nodded. "They gave me seven pints of

blood in the hospital. That's significant blood loss. They'll say I was impaired."

"Okay. I'll see what I think about your answers. When you first saw the senator, how would you describe his demeanor?"

"Dani and I had been running and hiding all night during the storm, from Ernest Yeoman's men." Harte made a vague gesture toward the case file in front of her. "By dawn, the storm had finally passed over and they were closing in on us. We were literally out of options when I finally recognized a landmark that I knew was close to my aunt Claire's house. My cousin Paul let us in and after we told him what was happening, Stamps appeared out of the shadows. He said he'd gone there for dinner the night before and gotten caught in the storm. He acted reluctant for us to know he was there."

Kate asked, "Reluctant?"

Harte nodded. "We'd been there for several minutes talking to Paul before Stamps stepped forward. It was as if he'd listened to us and decided it was okay for us to see him. So I guess I'd describe him as cautious and condescending. He started talking about how 'our city wasn't ready for more tragedy.' He was referring to the storm damage, of course."

"It *was* awful," Kate said. "A lot of houses on my street were badly damaged. My power was out all night, but I was lucky compared to a lot of other people."

Harte nodded. "Wasn't much fun being out in it," he said.

"I can't even imagine. Danielle Canto apparently handled it okay."

Upon hearing her name, Harte beamed and blushed at the same time. "Dani's a trouper," he said, unable to keep a smile from his face.

Kate didn't need her degree in psychiatry to read him at that moment. He was head over heels in love with Danielle Canto. "I didn't mean to interrupt," she said. "Please go ahead."

"Dani gave Stamps a hard time, asking him if he were practicing sound bites for the next election cycle. She reminded him that she'd heard the men who had killed her grandfather using his and Paul's names, as well as Ernest Yeoman's, when they had threatened him. Paul denied any involvement and seemed about to turn on Stamps. Then Stamps yelled, *Shut up,* and lunged at him."

"I saw that in Dani's statement. Did you hear him yourself?"

Harte nodded. "By that time I was pretty weak and hurting like a son of a bitch, but I was conscious. I definitely witnessed the exchange."

"Is that when Mr. Guillame sustained the gunshot wound?"

Harte shook his head. "No. That was later, after the gunmen broke in."

"Who else heard what Stamps said? Was your aunt Claire there? I don't see any mention of her."

"No. She's in Paris. Paul is house-sitting for her." Harte smiled wryly. "Has been for the past twenty years."

"So it was just you and Dani and Stamps and Paul Guillame in the house at that time?"

"That's right. Paul heard him, too, of course. But he's changed his story about what happened that night."

"Changed his story? How?" Kate shuffled through the files until she found the one labeled *Paul Guillame*.

"I didn't witness this, but apparently, when the police talked to Paul at the scene, Paul accused Stamps of shooting him. But then when he made his written statement, he swore the shooting was an accident. He said something like 'in the chaos, when the bullets started flying, Stamps must have shot him accidentally.'"

Kate tapped the eraser end of a pencil on her desk. "I saw in Miss Canto's statement that she described Stamps as furious. So was it an accident?"

"It doesn't sound like an accident." Harte gestured toward Dani's file. "Dani thought, because of what Stamps had yelled at Paul, that he was terrified Paul was about to incriminate Stamps, maybe even implicate himself, in Freeman Canto's death. But about that time the gunmen broke in and started shooting. While the bullets were flying, Stamps took the opportunity that presented itself to him. But that's going to be hard to prove. As I said before, I'm not a reliable witness and Dani, although she'd never lie, will be suspect, because of what she had heard on the night her granddad was murdered."

"Either way, his attorney is pushing for a finding of temporary insanity," Kate said, then gestured toward the envelope that Harte had delivered. "Apparently, she found a physician who's willing to testify that it was possible."

"I've never been involved with a temporary-insanity case. Isn't that nearly impossible to prove?" Harte asked. "I know one thing it does is shift the burden of proof from the prosecution to the defense."

"Which is always more difficult for the defense. And yes, it's very difficult to prove. I don't understand why a respected state senator would want to go that route, rather than just pleading innocent, if he and Guillame both are claiming it was an accident."

"He only fired once," Harte said. "My brother Lucas—he was the detective on the scene—

told me that Stamps's gun was missing only one round and they only found one casing that matched it. A very good case can be made that one deliberate gunshot argues against it being an accident." Harte paused, looking thoughtful. "If he were to plead innocent and be convicted of assault with intent or even simple assault, he'd be barred from holding public office forever."

"He's seventy-eight. How much longer do you think he plans to serve?" Kate asked.

Harte shrugged carefully, favoring his left shoulder. "Politicians have continued in office into their nineties and beyond. Look at Strom Thurmond or Robert Byrd."

"Okay," Kate said. "So he doesn't want to risk a guilty plea. Temporary insanity is going to put him under psychiatric care. Will that cause any issues with his senate seat?"

"He won't be allowed to serve while he's under court-appointed psychiatric care, but there's no reason he can't run again once he's released. There's no law against being crazy."

"No, there's not." Kate nodded. "Well, thanks for the information. I haven't examined the senator yet. I wanted to read through the case files first. As soon as I'm done, I'll get with the D.A."

Harte stood, said goodbye and left. Kate

watched him walk out. Even with an injury, he carried himself with dignity and grace, like Travis.

She rubbed her temple. Where were these thoughts of Travis coming from? Just from reading his brothers' and cousins' names in the police files and seeing his younger brother? That had to be it. She hardly ever thought about Travis during work these days. The times that she couldn't help but think about him were at night when she tucked Max in, or early in the morning when he ran into her room to *nuggle* under the covers with her, or when he begged for homemade *pasketti,* which was not only his favorite meal but his dad's, too.

She almost wished she'd asked Harte about his brother. But nobody in Travis's family except his younger sister, Cara Lynn, knew that she and Travis had dated. And even Cara Lynn didn't know that her brother was Max's father. She suspected, but she'd never asked and Kate had never told her.

Kate went back to reading Harte's statement. She didn't look up again until four o'clock, when Alice called out that she was leaving.

"Okay. I'm not far behind you," she responded. "Max is probably giving them fits at his day care. I made the mistake of telling them I was coming by early right in front of him. I'll see you tomorrow." She stood and stretched. Her muscles were a little tight from sitting in the same position and reading files all day. She put the files pertaining to the Stamps case in her briefcase, in case she had a chance to look at them after Max went to sleep, then walked into the outer office to get a drink of water from the cooler.

Her stomach growled. Two long swallows of cold water didn't quite make up for the yogurt and apple she'd forgotten to eat. She smiled to herself. She'd make *pasketti* tonight. Max would be thrilled. *Shrek* and *pasketti*. As she took another swallow of water, she heard her cell phone ring. She ran back into her office, blotting a drop of water off her chin with a finger, and grabbed it. "Hello?" she said.

"Dr. Chalmet." It was the voice from that morning.

Kate stiffened.

"This threat is anonymous, but it is not empty, Dr. Chalmet."

Her pulse quickened. The voice, which had sounded a bit hesitant in the earlier phone call, now had a ring of ominous confidence. She clutched the cell phone more tightly and listened without speaking.

"Someone who loves you very much is in

danger. You'll find out more very soon. But shh," the voice whispered, sending terror arrowing through her. "Don't tell anyone—not *anyone.* Don't go anywhere except to work and home. Don't talk to anybody, and keep your cell phone with you. Got that?"

"What? No, wait."

"Don't tell anyone, Dr. Chalmet, or he'll be gone forever." *Click.*

Kate stood frozen in place, with the faceless voice echoing in her ears. She hardly noticed when her phone slid from her fingers and hit the floor with a clatter. She collapsed into her desk chair as the voice's awful last words burned into her mind like a brand.

He'll be gone forever. Forever.

"No," she whispered. "No, no, no." She had to do something. She looked at her empty hand. Why was it empty?

Her phone. She'd been holding her phone. She slid out of the chair and felt around on the floor, desperate to find it. Her fingers encountered a thin piece of plastic, then a small flat thing, then the body of the phone. The back and the battery had been knocked off when it had hit the floor. With hands that shook so much she could barely hold the pieces, she put the phone back together, then stared at the dark screen for several seconds before she realized she needed to turn it on.

She pressed the correct button and the display came on. There was no information about the call. Just the words *Private Number.*

Her thumb trembled over the 9 key. She had to call 9-1-1. Didn't she? So they could trace the call and stop the man before he had a chance to grab Max?

He'll be gone forever.

Max! Day care! He was at day care! She had to call them—make sure he was still there. Tell them she was on her way.

She tried to page down to their number, but her fingers wouldn't work right. She tried again, carefully pushing the buttons. Finally, she was looking at the number. But before she could press Call, her office phone rang.

Her head snapped up and she realized she was still on her knees on the floor. She pulled herself to her feet. Reaching for the phone's handset, she stopped with her hand less than an inch away. She couldn't make herself pick it up. She couldn't talk to anyone. She had to get to Max. But what if it was the day care? What if it was that man again? She had to answer it.

Finally she wrapped her fingers around the handset and lifted it to her ear. "Hello?" she rasped.

"Dr. Chalmet? This is Missy at Bluebird Day Care. We've had an incident." Missy's voice trembled. "I have a n-note on the schedule that you were going to pick Max up early today. Have you already picked him up?"

Kate's throat closed as panic sent a flash of heat through her. She felt as though she'd been struck by lightning. She couldn't speak. She couldn't even breathe. *Gone forever.* She tried to swallow and couldn't. She opened her mouth but nothing came out.

"Dr. Chalmet?" Missy said, her voice half an octave higher now and tinged with panic.

Kate forced her scattered mind into a semblance of focus. She had to say something—had to do this. Her child's life was at stake.

"I— Yes," she said, her hand at her throat, amazed that she'd managed to squeeze any sound past the constriction there. *Max! My little Max. Dear God, don't let them hurt him.*

"I…did." Had she even said that aloud? She still felt as if no breath could escape her throat.

Missy let out a deep sigh. "You did? Oh, thank God!" she said. "I am *so* sorry, Dr. Chalmet. I know what you must think, me calling you like this. It's just that we had such a scare."

Kate's hand throbbed with pain—that's how hard she was gripping the handset. She stood like a statue, looking at nothing, listening as the young woman named Missy told her exactly how the anonymous caller had abducted Max.

"The smoke alarms went off and we smelled smoke, so we evacuated the building. The children were all fine. All accounted for. Once we discovered that there was no fire, we started gathering them up to take them back inside. It was then—less than five minutes ago—that I realized I didn't see Max. I'm outside right now, on my cell. I've been looking all over for him. I can't tell you how relieved I am that you have him. Did you just drive by and see him and pick him up?"

"Y-yes," Kate said, thankful that she didn't have to think up an explanation. "I did. I—I was about to call you."

"That's what I thought. I was so scared. I was going to call the police."

"No!" Kate snapped hoarsely.

"Ma'am?"

Kate cleared her throat. "Sorry. I—dropped something. But no—don't call the police," she said, hearing herself speaking higher and faster. She took a deep breath and pressed her hand over her mouth before she spoke again. "He's—he's fine."

"Dr. Chalmet, are you sure everything's all right?"

Kate gathered strength from somewhere—

she had no idea where. All she knew was, if this woman became suspicious, she'd call the police, and if she did—

He'll be gone forever.

"Yes, yes, of course. I'm fine. Ev-everything's fine. I've got company and my—my cookies are burning. I appreciate you checking on Max."

"Yes, ma'am. Again, I am so sorry. Believe me, this will never happen again. Please understand."

"Thank you. I do. I have to go," Kate said in her doctor-knows-best voice. She heard the click on the other end of the phone. She placed the handset carefully and quietly into the cradle.

Then, very slowly, she crumpled to the floor, clutching her cell phone against her stomach.

Chapter Two

Travis parked in front of Kate's house. He sat there in the dark, feeling the trembling in his limbs that signaled exhaustion. It wasn't something he'd ever felt until he'd been captured. And since he'd been shipped back to the U.S., it had been his constant companion.

He'd been so anxious to get to New Orleans that he'd only stopped once during the thousand-mile journey from Bethesda. He'd pulled into a rest area and slept for about four hours, waking in a panic every time an 18-wheeler had roared past or a car had honked or backfired.

He hadn't thought about what he would do once he got to Kate's house, he realized. Every time he'd thought about her—during his captivity, in the hospital, as he was buying this *little beauty*—he'd pictured himself at her door, waiting for her to open it.

He had no clue what he would say once he was face-to-face with her.

Right now, even though he was almost thirty, the temptation to drive across the lake to his parents' house and let his mom take care of him was nearly irresistible. Her gentle nature and subtle but ironclad will would be welcome right now. He was exhausted and angry and confused, and she'd know exactly what to do to make him feel better.

But he couldn't afford to let his family know where he was—not yet. He wanted to see Kate first. And now, here he was.

He took a deep breath and reached up to rub his stubbled cheek. He felt his arm muscles tremble at the small exertion. He blew out a frustrated breath. Was part of the shakiness caused by the anticipation of seeing her? One way or another, he had to rebuild his strength.

He reached for the car door handle. He'd go to the door, tell her what he came to tell her, then get a room for the night. At a decent hour in the morning, he'd go to his parents' house. If he really pleaded with his mom, he could convince her not to tell anyone he was home. Then in a few days, he'd figure out what his next step should be. The one thing he knew was that there was no way he'd go back to Walter Reed or to any other hospital.

He walked up to Kate's front door, thinking it was probably a good sign that the only car in the driveway was the Accord, the same car she'd had five years ago. If she had a man in her life, it appeared he wasn't here.

Travis squeezed his hands into fists, flexed his fingers, then knocked on the door and waited.

Nothing happened. He glanced at the windows. He didn't hear any movement, didn't see any lights flash on. The one dim light, which looked like a lamp in the living room, remained the only light on in the house.

He knocked again, his brain suddenly filled with all the reasons why she wasn't answering the door. Why hadn't he thought of all this earlier?

There *was* a man and they had gone out in his car.

She was asleep, although at eight-thirty that didn't seem likely.

She was in the back of the house and hadn't heard him knock.

She'd recognized him through the window and didn't want to open the door.

Then he heard something. He took a step back, his hands at his sides like a schoolboy, and waited to see the face that had kept him from losing his mind during those five long months in captivity.

K ATE STARED AT the doorknob through blurry, tear-swollen eyes. Her first thought when she'd heard the knock was that the police had found Max and brought him home. She'd almost fainted with relief. Then it occurred to her that the young woman from the day care might have seen through her desperate lies and had called the cops to report her child missing.

"No, please. Just don't be the police," she whispered as she opened the door, praying for the best but bracing herself for the worst. She clung to the knob as she tried to see who was standing in the shadows beyond the dim porch light.

Suddenly, a third possibility rose in her brain. This could be Max's abductor, here to tell her what he wanted her to do. Her breath hitched. Maybe he'd have Max with him.

She pressed a palm against her chest and stared at the dark figure that stood just beyond the light. She blinked, but she still couldn't see into the darkness. "Who is it?" she asked, trying to sound confident, but hearing the hoarse fear in her voice.

The figure moved forward so that the light played across his features. Kate frowned, trying to make sense of what she saw. "H-Harte?" she stammered, taking in the familiar hard edge of the man's jaw. "Is that you?"

"Kate?"

The voice was ragged and hesitant. Kate frowned and squinted. The body was whipcord thin with long, sinewy muscles. No, it wasn't Harte—but everything about the figure was so familiar. Who could it be? Her brain whirled, trying to make sense of what her eyes saw. There were two older Delancey brothers who were cops. Was this one of them, come to tell her something about Max? Terror ripped through her heart. The police rarely came to the door with good news.

The figure took another step forward, enough so that the light caught his dark, intense eyes.

"Oh my God," she whispered. There was no mistaking those eyes. "How—? Where—?" Suddenly she couldn't breathe. She clutched at her chest. She felt light-headed. Then her knees collapsed. "Travis?"

TRAVIS CAUGHT KATE as she swayed. He staggered under her weight. Not that she was heavy. He was just so damned weak. He half carried her to the couch and sat her down. There were drops of sweat on her forehead and she was

pale as a ghost. But that didn't make sense.
Kate had always been the epitome of control.
She wouldn't faint. She wasn't the type.

He sat on the coffee table and looked at her
closely. He'd noticed how pale she was as soon
as she'd opened the door. Now he saw that the
skin around her eyes was puffy and red. She'd
been crying, and that wasn't like her, either.
Something was desperately wrong with her.
And the one thing he was sure of was that it
had nothing to do with him.

She stirred and opened her eyes. It didn't
matter how red and swollen they were. Those
aquamarine eyes were stunning. She stared
blankly for a few seconds as if she weren't
looking at him at all. Then she took a deep
breath that hitched at the top like a sob and
sat up.

"Travis?" she said tentatively. Her hand
lifted toward him.

He caught it in his. "Hey," he said, smiling at her. To his horror, her face crumpled
and she started crying, pulling her hand away.
The crying was a tortured, desperate weeping, totally silent, except for the short, sobbing breaths. Tears streamed down her cheeks,
which already appeared chapped. She clasped
her hands, the fingers intertwining like a nest
of snakes.

Travis felt impotent, helpless. He had no idea what was the matter with her and no idea what to do. But he knew all this was a lot more than just a reaction from seeing him at her door. He went to the kitchen to get her a glass of water. In the dim light from the one lamp, he stumbled over something on the floor. He looked in the cabinet for a glass, pushing aside small, colorful plastic cups with cartoon logos on them to reach a tumbler. He navigated a maze of plastic things on the floor to get back to the couch.

She'd blotted her tears with the cuff of her suit jacket and was sitting calmly. Every so often a little sob would shake her.

After handing her the water, Travis sat down on the coffee table again, avoiding a big pile of picture books and DVDs. He watched as Kate drank the water. Once it was gone, he took the glass and set it down beside him.

Her gaze locked to his. "What—what are you doing here?" she asked, entwining her fingers again and squeezing until the knuckles turned white.

"Doesn't matter," he said. "What's wrong with you? Has something happened?"

"Oh," she gasped, pressing both hands to her chest as if the pain there was too much to bear.

"Kate, tell me."

He watched her gather strength from somewhere. She sat up and wiped the tears away from her face, then took a deep breath. It still hitched slightly, but she ignored it. "They've taken Max," she said. Her gaze wavered for a second. "My son."

Her words hit Travis like a blow to the gut. "Your what?" he said stupidly, as his brain repeated what she'd said. *They've taken Max. My son.* If he had any further doubt that he'd misheard, the look on Kate's face convinced him. She was terrified and sick with worry. No wonder she'd collapsed.

Then, suddenly, something clicked in his brain. All the things he'd been dodging and tripping over since he had come into the house suddenly made sense. The plastic things on the floor were toys and the picture books and DVDs on the coffee table were children's stories. Now the little neon-bright cups with cartoon logos made sense, as well.

"Who, Kate? Who took him?" He wanted to ask more questions, different ones. *Whose son is he? Why didn't you let me know? Where's his father now, when you need him?* But those questions could wait.

"I don't know," she said desperately. "They— The man called."

"Have you phoned the police?" he asked, knowing the answer. If she had, they'd be here.

"No, no, no," she said, shaking her head. "If I do, he'll be gone forever." She wasn't crying now. She sat still, stiff as a board, and kept her eyes on her hands clasped in her lap. "He said so."

Travis took them in his. "Listen to me, Kate. Whatever they told you, whatever you think they might do, we have to call the police. They know how to deal with these things—"

"No!" she snapped, pulling away. "No police! I just have to do what they say. It'll all be over soon if I just do what they say."

"You said you don't know who they are?"

She shook her head. "No, but I know what they want. All I have to do is declare that Myron Stamps was temporarily insane at the time of the shooting, so he can be acquitted. Then they'll bring Max home." She nodded. "They will—" her breath hitched again "—won't they?"

"I don't know, Kate." Travis studied her. "Look, I'll call Lucas—my oldest brother. He's a detective with NOPD. He'll know what to do."

"No!" she cried, vaulting up. Her face was a mask of desperate fear. "I said no. You can't say anything to anybody. They'll kill my baby. They said so." She wrung her hands. "Please."

"Okay." He held up his hands in a gesture of surrender.

She stared at him suspiciously, tears glittering in her eyes. "Please, Travis. You have to promise me you won't say anything." She wrung her hands. "Oh, why did I tell you? They said if I told anyone— I was just so surprised to see you standing there."

Travis remembered what she'd said when she had first seen his face. His chest felt as if a massive fist had reached in and squeezed his heart. "You said my brother's name when you first opened the door. I didn't think you knew any of my family. Is Harte—?" His voice quit on him.

"What? Harte?" She stared at him uncomprehendingly.

"Is he—?" He gestured vaguely around. "Is he your son's—?"

Understanding lit her blue eyes. Understanding and frustration. She frowned. "No! Of course not. I know Harte from the D.A.'s office."

Travis waited but Kate didn't offer up any further explanation. He didn't want to pry— Lord knew he had no right to—but he needed to know one thing. "Kate, does your son's father know? Is he coming?"

She looked up at him, then back down at her hands. "No."

"What about your family? Any of them coming down to help you?"

"I haven't called anybody. Didn't you hear what I told you? They said not to tell *anyone*."

"Yet you told me," he said quietly.

She nodded dejectedly. "And now I wish I hadn't. I didn't mean to. You—surprised me." She gasped. "What if they're watching the house? They'll think you're the police. They'll think I called you. You have to go." She shot to her feet and grabbed his shirtsleeve. "Get up. You have to get out of here, right now, before they find out you're here."

Travis stood. "Kate, calm down." He took her hand off his sleeve and held it. "I'm not leaving you here by yourself."

"No!" she snapped, jerking her hand away. "You don't understand. They will *kill* him. *Kill him*. You have to go. Go!"

"Kate, listen to me." Travis wrapped his fingers around her upper arms. "You've got to calm down right now. You're panicking and not thinking straight. We need to think about this rationally. Figure out the best thing to do. I'll guarantee you one thing. I am *not* leaving you here alone."

Kate just squeezed her arms tighter around

herself. "But what about Max? I can't take the chance—"

"Think about it. They're not going to hurt him. They know that the only reason you'll agree to help them is to save your son. They wouldn't dare do anything to him now."

She stared at him and slowly, under his fingers, her arm muscles relaxed. "They won't? How do you know that?"

"They don't have a choice. They have to make sure he's safe and cared for." God he hoped he was right. The people who had taken her child weren't asking her to decide if someone lived or died. All they wanted was for her to say that some guy had been temporarily insane when he'd shot someone. Surely they had no intention of harming the child. Now, if he could only make her believe it.

She nodded.

He breathed a sigh of relief. "Good. Now I'm going to call Lucas—"

She grabbed his hand, digging her nails into his palm. "No! I told you, no police!"

"I thought we agreed they're not going to hurt him."

"Travis, I hope you're right," she said, those aquamarine eyes staring intensely into his. "I pray you are, but until my baby is back in my arms, I have to believe what they told me. I am not telling anyone anything."

He knew that look in her eyes and that tone of voice. She'd reached her limit. She wouldn't budge.

He shrugged. "Okay. Well, you're not getting rid of me. I don't care if I have to camp on your lawn—I'm not leaving you to face this alone."

Her face fell apart again. Her eyes closed and she swayed. Travis caught her and pulled her into his arms. Holding her, taking care of her, was what he'd dreamed of during the long months he'd spent in captivity. Dreamed of, but never believed would happen. He'd been afraid he would die in that hellhole. So he'd fortified himself and stayed sane by reliving his memories of the people he loved.

He was holding the best part of those memories in his arms right now, but his reasons for coming here no longer mattered. Kate's limp, trembling body was testament to the torture she was experiencing. Her child was missing. His goal now was to lend her what little strength he had and help her find her little boy. He held her, trying to ignore the familiar strawberry scent of her hair and the firm yet soft feel of her body against his.

Finally she straightened and pushed against him, ready to stand on her own two feet again.

"You okay?" he whispered, his mouth near her ear.

She nodded, sending another wave of strawberries across his nostrils.

"I'll let you stay here. I don't want to be by myself. Besides—" she lifted her head and looked into his eyes "—I have to keep an eye on you so you won't call in the entire Delancey police force."

He smiled grimly. Grasping her arms, he set her away from him. "I promise you I won't. Not until you and I both agree," he said, pointing at her then at himself to emphasize that he was being truthful. "Now on to more important things. You look exhausted. Why don't you take a shower and get ready for bed?"

She started shaking her head. "I can't sleep—"

He squeezed her arms and bent his head to look into her eyes. "You'd be surprised what you can do when you have no other choice," he said. "If you don't sleep, you'll lose strength and focus. Trust me, I know. You won't be able to think clearly enough to do your job."

She lifted her head. "You're right," she said. "I guess I will take a shower. What time is it?"

Travis glanced at his watch. "Nine-thirty. Are you going in to work tomorrow?"

She shook her head. "I'll have to pretend to

be sick. There's no way I can fool my secretary, Alice. She'll know something's wrong." As she talked, she took off the gray suit jacket and began unbuttoning her shirt, seemingly unaware that she was undressing right in front of him. Then she turned and walked out of the living room.

Travis watched her and swallowed hard as an image of her—wet, warm and naked from the shower—filled his inner vision. He'd always loved to touch her, to taste her, after her shower. Her skin always smelled and tasted like lavender, and her hair like strawberries.

His stomach growled, interrupting his thoughts. Just as well. He had no right to think of her like that. He deliberately turned his mind to practical things. He needed to eat something or he was going to collapse. He went into the kitchen and opened the refrigerator. There was a block of cheddar cheese, a carton of milk and several containers of yogurt, as well as about a dozen individually boxed juice drinks. He looked around and spotted half a loaf of bread. Grabbing a slice, he wrapped it around a couple slices of cheese. Picking up the milk carton, he sniffed it. It was fine. Milk probably didn't last long enough to go bad with a kid around. He poured himself a glass, then leaned against the refrigerator and ate.

BY THE TIME he'd forced down half of the sandwich, Kate came out into the living room in a terry-cloth robe. The hot water hadn't helped her swollen eyes much, but she did look more comfortable and somewhat more relaxed.

"You look like you feel a little better," he said.

Kate stared at Travis, leaning against her refrigerator as if he belonged there. How had he materialized at her door on this of all nights? The hot shower had drained the last dregs of energy out of her, but as she looked at him, it occurred to her that he looked worse than she did. He was pale and drawn. His clothes hung loose on his frame and there were dark circles under his eyes.

He saluted her with the glass. "I helped myself. Hope that's okay."

"Sure," Kate said. "I just need enough milk for Max's—" She stopped and put her hand over her mouth, trying to stifle the moan that burned in her throat. She hunched her shoulders against the pain that settled under her breastbone. "I keep forgetting he's not here. I can't stand it," she whispered. "What am I going to do?"

"It's going to be okay, Kate. I promise."

"Is it?" she said. "I don't like empty words. You know that."

His mouth thinned. "Yet you're asking empty questions. You know what you should do. I'm not suggesting you call 9-1-1 and have police cars racing over here with sirens blazing. But if you'd let me call Lucas or Ethan, they could help you. They'll know how to deal with a kidnapping."

Kate stiffened and clenched her fists. "I said no," she snapped. "We are talking about my son's life. I have to be able to trust you, because if I can't, then—" She stopped. Then what? He already knew Max had been kidnapped. He could call his brothers anytime. For all she knew he already had.

"Did you call anybody while I was in the shower?"

He shook his head, looking down at the empty glass in his hand as if he didn't remember that he had it. Then he turned and set it on the kitchen counter.

His behavior pulled her out of her haze of terror for Max's safety. "Your brothers? Your parents?"

He shook his head again without raising his head. "I said no. I just drove up," he muttered.

Just drove up? He'd driven straight here from—from who knew where. "Why? I mean, why are you here?"

He shrugged. He looked at the cheese sandwich he held and made a face, then set it down next to the glass.

He was being evasive. She knew he was in the elite Special Forces division of the army. Was he here on another furlough, hoping to hook up with her again, just like five years ago? Or on sick leave? Maybe he'd been wounded. She didn't understand much about Special Forces, but she did know they drew the hardest missions in the most dangerous places on the planet. "So are you on sick leave?"

His head shot up. "Why would you say that?"

"Come on, Trav, it's obvious you've lost a lot of weight. You look awful."

He gave her a crooked smile that didn't even begin to touch his dark eyes. "Thanks."

"You know what I mean. In case you've forgotten, I'm a psychiatrist. I have a medical degree. You didn't think I wouldn't notice, did you?"

His eyes narrowed and his chin lifted. "No. I knew you would. I—" He swallowed. "They gave me some leave and I didn't want Mom to see me. Not till I put some weight back on."

Kate stared at him, almost wanting to smile. He'd always been the worst liar on the face of the earth. He looked as though he should be in the hospital. He had on a long-sleeved shirt, but she'd bet a month's salary that she'd find an IV stick point on his arm. "No," she said, shaking her head. "No, they didn't give you leave. You left AMA, didn't you?"

"What?" he said, but he evaded her gaze. "AMA?"

"You know what it means. Against medical advice. You were in the hospital, weren't you?"

"We're not talking about me. You need to decide. Do you want me here or not? I can go stay with Lucas. He'll understand that I don't want to see Mom and Dad—and no," he added quickly. "I won't tell him anything."

TRAVIS WATCHED her carefully, waiting to see what she'd do. He didn't want to have to explain why he'd come here. Not now. But he did want to stay. He wanted to be here for her during what must be the most awful few days in her life. Her child was missing. If he could help her, he would. If she'd let him.

"Well? Should I pitch a tent in your front yard?"

She shook her head tiredly. "No. Please stay." Then she straightened and gave a little nod. It was a gesture he knew very well. It meant she'd made up her mind. "I think I'll have some juice," she said evenly and stepped toward the refrigerator.

Travis backed away so she could get to it.

Despite his resolve, he couldn't help but admire her. She was still as beautiful as she'd always been. Beautiful, graceful, with a delicate outer shell that hid the steel inside her.

His gaze traveled over her from head to foot. She was barefoot, her toenails painted a delicate, sexy pink color. He swallowed, thinking ruefully that he must be exhausted, because, while he found it hard to take his eyes off her pretty toes, he was more interested in a hot shower and a comfortable bed than sex.

Shaking his head slightly, he picked up the sandwich and concentrated on taking one more bite. He had trouble washing it down. He hadn't felt like eating since he'd gotten back from overseas. And prior to that, while he'd been held captive, he'd been given barely enough food to keep him alive. Tonight, the cheese sandwich had been like manna from heaven. He wished he could have eaten more than half of it, but his shrunken stomach wouldn't let him.

"I'm glad you're here," she said hesitantly.

"I know," he responded, tossing the leftover sandwich in the trash. "Makes it easier for you to keep an eye on me. To make sure I don't go running to Lucas or Ethan."

"Well, that," she admitted with a small smile. "But also, it makes me feel safe."

It was a reflection of the state of his mind and his body that his first thought was relief that he wouldn't have to drive any more tonight. "You couldn't make me leave if you tried," he said wryly.

Her smile faded. "Travis, you never answered my question. What are you doing here? Why did you show up here tonight?" Her gaze grew sharp.

"It's kind of a long story, Kate. Why don't we talk about it later? Right now, you need to get some sleep. And I need to take a shower and get some sleep myself. I've got a bag in the car."

She nodded, still pondering him.

As she sat down on the couch, he headed out to his car to get his duffel bag. When he returned, Kate pointed him toward Max's room, which was filled with more toys, as well as stuffed animals and books. He grabbed a pair of sweatpants and a T-shirt and headed to the bathroom. By the time he was finished showering, the hot water had made him so drowsy he could barely hold his eyes open.

He walked out into the living room and found Kate asleep on the couch, the remote control for the television held loosely in her hand. Her lips were parted. Her soft breaths were barely audible. He was glad to see she'd fallen asleep. The last thing he wanted to do was to wake her. But he didn't want to leave her here in the dark by herself, either.

He took the remote and set it on the coffee table, then grabbed an afghan from the back of an armchair and gently spread it over her. When he turned out the lights and sat next to her, she turned and snuggled up against him. A lump grew in his throat as he relaxed back against the soft couch cushions.

He'd fled the confines of a military hospital and the shrinks who were trying to treat him for an illness that he didn't believe he had. He'd traveled twenty-four hours to see her— maybe to clear his conscience by telling her he still loved her, maybe in hopes that she would want him back.

But his motive for coming here was no longer important. When she'd opened her front door, he'd walked right into her nightmare. He didn't understand much about what was going on—not yet. But he knew one thing. Kate needed his help, and whatever he could do to help her find her child, he'd do it with all the strength he had in him.

Chapter Three

"Can't you shut that kid up?" Bentley Woods groaned as he turned over on the narrow, lumpy sofa. "It's hard enough to sleep on this damn fleabag couch without having to listen to him whining." For a few seconds he didn't hear anything except the kid's caterwauling.

Then the bedroom door opened and Shirley stuck her straw-blond head out. "Shh!" she hissed. "If you don't stop yelling, I'll never get him to sleep."

"What's the matter with him, anyhow? I thought kids slept a lot." Bent sat up and groped for a cigarette. He lit it with a disposable lighter and took a deep pull.

"That shows how much you know about kids," Shirley said, slipping through the door and closing it quietly. Behind it, the kid sniffled. "Maybe he misses his mama."

Bent snorted. "He'll miss her a lot more if she doesn't cooperate."

"Oh, give me a break. You're not going to hurt that kid or his mama." Shirley leaned over the back of the couch and kissed his forehead.

"I will if I have to."

"You get squeamish if you have to use your gun. Call me, you big wuss. I'll shoot her."

"You are good," he said, smirking at her.

"You bet your life. Now gimme a hit on that cigarette."

"Get your own," he retorted.

"I can't smoke in there. That's not healthy for him."

"You're coddling that squirt. Since when are you all interested in babies?"

Shirley grabbed his cigarette and drew deeply on it, then handed it back. "Since you informed me I had to babysit one. And he's four years old—hardly a baby." Smoke drifted out of her mouth as she spoke.

"Four years, four months. What's the difference?"

She laughed. "About a dozen dirty diapers a day," she said.

"Whatever. Why don't you give him some more cough medicine, so I can get some sleep?"

Shirley tossed her head. Her curly blond hair didn't move. "Can't. He's already had a full dose. It's easy to give a little kid like that too much. He'll go to sleep soon."

"Hey," Bent said, cocking his head as he blew smoke out through his nose. "I don't hear him. Looks like he's happier when you're not in the room. Why don't you bring him out here, or make him a pallet on the floor in that back room. Then you and me can take the bedroom. I can't sleep on this broken-down thing every night by myself. I'll never get any sleep."

Shirley took his cigarette and inhaled another puff, then blew it out. "Too bad. It was your brilliant idea to bring me down here to take care of this kid for you, so just shut up and let me do it. How long before we can give him back to his mama and head back to Chicago?"

"I told you, the trial's supposed to start in ten days. Once those country bumpkins have their ruling of insanity, they'll tell me where to leave him and pick up my money. All we got to do is make sure nothing happens to him."

"I can take care of him," Shirley said, her hand on her hip as she stood near the bedroom door. "I took care of three little brothers. Your problem's going to be keeping *me* happy. Especially if I have to stay cooped up here all day, every day." She pointed a finger at Bent. "Next time you go out, I want a steak. A big one. And get me a bottle of good burgundy. If I gotta do this, I'm at least gonna eat good."

Bent put out his cigarette and turned over

and pressed his nose into the couch cushions. "You eat good every day," he grumbled. "You better watch out. One day you're going to wake up fat."

"Yeah. Hold your breath. No wait, don't. You might have a heart attack, Mister 'Bring Me a Big Mac.'" She put her hand on the doorknob. "If the kid's bothering you, go sleep in that back room yourself. Or better yet, the car." She eased the door open and slipped back into the bedroom, closing it behind her.

"Better yet, the car," Bent mocked quietly. He could hear her cooing and whispering to the little boy he'd been hired to kidnap. No matter how much he complained, he had to admit that Shirley was good with the little rug rat.

Damn, he'd be glad when this backwoods job was over. He'd taken it on as a favor—well, that and for the dough. Much as he complained, he was getting good money. He ought to be, considering this hellhole. He was used to holing up in out-of-the-way places. But he didn't think he'd ever been as out of the way as he was in this disgusting little trailer park, surrounded by people whose talk he couldn't understand and who did things that were just plain weird. What was the deal with fishing with nothing but a pole and cockroaches? Ugh! Or digging up the nasty creatures they called crawfish.

He grunted and wriggled, looking for a comfortable position on the dilapidated couch. There wasn't one. He hated the South. He hated Louisiana. He hated this damn ugly trailer park. The whole county smelled of fish, mud and sweat. Still, he figured he could stand anything for another ten days. Especially at this price tag. He laughed harshly as he lit another cigarette. Good thing they weren't spending too much money on accommodations.

All he had to do was keep an eye on the mom. It was Shirley's job to watch the kid. Bent would be spending all day and evening watching the doctor, making sure she didn't try to go to the police, and all night trying to sleep. As soon as the doctor testified that some blustery old politician was crazy, they could give the kid back and get the hell out of this sweat-hole.

The man who had hired him had a vested interest in keeping the old guy out of prison. Bent didn't know what that reason was and he didn't care. He just wanted his money in his pocket and his tires back on the road to Chicago—for good.

He squinted at his watch. Almost one o'clock in the morning. He wiggled around again, cursing under his breath. He hadn't had a good night's sleep since he had gotten here three days ago. Holding his breath, he listened. Damn if the kid hadn't quieted down. Maybe he could get some shut-eye now. He sighed and closed his eyes.

Then, through the closed door, Bent heard the kid yell, "I want my mom-eeee...!"

Groaning, he grabbed a throw pillow and jammed it over his head.

THE FIRST THING Kate thought when she woke up was that the horror of the day before had just been a bad dream. Then she opened her eyes and realized that she was not in her bed. She was on the couch in the living room and there was someone beside her.

For a few seconds, she tried to ignore her senses. Tried to stay in that netherworld between asleep and awake, where everything was just as it should be. Where Max was snuggled up beside her, safe and secure.

Max. She fell out of the dream world with a jolt. The nauseating fear that roiled up from her stomach like bile was no dream. It was all too real.

It wasn't Max next to her. Her sweet baby was in the hands of strangers, scared and alone, crying for her. Probably thinking she'd gone off and left him. Her eyes, still swollen and sore, stung anew with tears. She pressed her hand against her chest, where her heart felt ripped to shreds. How was she going to bear the pain until this was all over? She had no one she could go to, no one to look to for help. She knew what would happen if she told anyone.

The person beside her breathed deeply, drawing her attention. She remembered. It was Travis. What miracle had brought him to her door the night before?

She didn't know why he was here, but she did know he could help her. He was strong and smart. And he was a Green Beret. There was nothing he couldn't do.

She didn't want to wake him, so she shifted carefully, until she could look at his face. She hadn't paid much attention to how he'd looked last night. She'd had a hard enough time coping with the shock of seeing him on top of the shock of finding out her child had been abducted.

Now she studied him. The best thing she could say was that he looked awful. She couldn't see his dark eyes, since he was asleep. But his ridiculously long eyelashes, which his son had inherited from him, rested on the purple circles below his eyes. His cheeks were hollow, where Max's were adorably plump, but there was no doubt that they were father and son.

She scanned his long, lean body. He was so thin. Of course, he'd never been bulky. At six feet one inch, he had the body of a basketball player or a swimmer. Lean but rock hard.

He must have lost twenty pounds. Had he been sick? She had no idea where he'd been or what he'd been doing for the past five years. He could have been sitting pretty behind a desk or stuck in a dark prison for all she knew.

Then she noticed a red line above his right eyebrow. Was that a scar? Now that she was looking for them, she spotted other small marks on his face—at the corner of his lip, on the curve of his jaw, at his hairline.

He opened his eyes. Kate gasped in surprise. She'd leaned forward as she studied his face, and now their lips were less than three inches apart. He lifted a hand and touched her hair.

Something happened inside her chest. A fluttering. She recognized it. She'd felt that same sensation every time he'd touched her back in college, and nothing had changed since she had seen him five years ago during his furlough.

The years fell away and her brain was suddenly sending her screen shots of all their good times together. Then Travis pushed his fingers through her hair and pushed all thoughts out of her head. He tugged gently, pulling her head down until he could reach her lips. "Morning, Kate," he murmured, then kissed her lightly.

She swallowed. "Morning," she said, looking into his dark eyes. His gaze held hers for a moment, then slid downward to look at her lips. He leaned forward again and touched her mouth with his. She closed her eyes. It felt so familiar, his hands in her hair, his mouth on hers.

But what was she doing? Her Max was gone. She pulled away, shaking her head, her eyes filling with tears.

Travis let go of her and sat back. "How'd you sleep?" he asked, his gaze roaming over her features.

She bit her lip and blinked against the tears.

"I was dreaming about Max. When I woke up, I thought he was here, snuggled up against me. I thought that yesterday was the bad dream."

He nodded solemnly.

She got up. "Do you want some coffee?" she asked.

"Yeah," he said as he pushed himself to his feet. "Please."

Kate watched him walk across the living room and into the hall, headed for the bathroom. He moved stiffly, like a patient weak from surgery. But still, his long bones and sleek muscles gave him the unconscious grace and dignity that was so familiar to her.

She felt stiff herself. Her back ached. Obviously, sleeping half sitting, half lying down on a couch was not good for a body. By the time Travis came back into the living room, Kate had the coffee going. He sat at the kitchen counter.

"Tell me about this court case," he said as she held out a steaming mug. To her surprise, his hands trembled as he took it. She glanced up at his face, but his eyes were on the coffee. He lifted it to his mouth and took a cautious sip. "Mmm. It's funny, the things you miss the most. That's good. Chicory?"

"Of course," she answered, smiling. "And boiled milk, plus plenty of sugar for you." She picked up her coffee mug and came around the counter to sit on a stool beside him.

"So who is it you're supposed to evaluate?"

"Myron Stamps. You should recognize the name. He's been in the legislature since forever."

"Stamps?" He shrugged. "I never paid much attention to politics. Seems like I've heard of him."

"What about Freeman Canto?"

"Oh sure. He and my granddad were big political rivals and friends back in the day."

"Right. Well, Canto was murdered a little over a year ago. His granddaughter was at home and heard the attack. She claims that the men who broke in kept repeating three names—Ernest Yeoman, Senator Stamps and Paul Guillame."

"Paul?" Travis laughed. "They yelled Paul's name? For what? Because I'll personally testify that Paul couldn't beat up a teddy bear."

"Your brother Harte caught the case. Oh—" She gasped, suddenly remembering Harte's injury. "Travis," she said, laying a hand on his forearm. "Harte was shot. In the chest!" At Travis's look of horror, she quickly amended, "I'm sorry. Of course he's fine. Almost as good as new."

"Harte—shot?"

She nodded. "He was shot by Yeoman's men, after he and Dani had been running and hiding from them all night during the storm."

Travis shook his head tiredly. "What? I'm totally lost. What's been going on and what does it all have to do with you—and your son?"

"I'm not sure I understand it all yet myself, but here's all I know. Your brother was holding Danielle Canto in protective custody until time came to testify in the trial of a local businessman named Ernest Yeoman. She had heard the men who killed her grandfather say Yeoman's name, as well as Stamps and Paul Guillame."

"Why were the men talking about Stamps and Paul?" Travis asked, still looking bewildered.

"The theory is that Stamps and a couple other local politicians were accepting bribes to keep the tariffs on imports low, to help smugglers. Apparently Yeoman has been suspected of smuggling in illegal imports for years."

"That doesn't explain Paul."

Kate shrugged. "I can't explain that. But the Friday before Yeoman's trial was to start, there was a huge storm—wind, lightning, flooding. Someone threw a Molotov cocktail and a smoke bomb through the window of the bed-and-breakfast where Danielle was staying, so they had to run. They ended up—"

"Wait. Who had to run?"

"Harte and Danielle. After hiding and running all night, they ended up at Paul Guillame's house. Apparently Harte was shot before they got to Paul's house. Once they were in the house, a shoot-out ensued and Stamps shot Paul. Yeoman was convicted of conspiracy to commit murder in Freeman Canto's death. I suppose Danielle's testimony about hearing Stamps's name wasn't enough to link him to the murder. But he's coming to trial for shooting Paul Guillame." She spread her hands. "Personally, I'm not completely clear on why the D.A. is pushing this so hard. I mean, Guillame even says it was an accident. But the D.A. is determined to prosecute Stamps. He wants me to tear down the defense's claim of temporary insanity. Now whoever is pushing for him to get off on a temporary-insanity plea has stolen my baby." Her breath hitched. She didn't know how much longer she could live without knowing whether Max was okay.

Travis shook his head as if shaking it would help all the information settle into his brain. "You're sure Harte's all right?"

She nodded. "He brought some papers over to my office yesterday morning. He said he was sore and tired but was feeling good otherwise." Then she smiled. "By the way, I'm pretty sure he and Danielle Canto are quite the item, after spending that entire night together hiding from the bad guys."

"Looks like I've missed a lot these past five years."

Kate's breath stuck in her throat. He had no idea how true his words were.

Travis finished his coffee and set the mug down. She noticed that he clasped his hands in front of him, probably to hide their trembling. She was a good doctor, but she didn't need a medical degree to see that something terrible had happened to him. The signs were obvious—weight loss, trembling, the weakness and the sunken eyes. He was suffering from PTSD, maybe brought on by the rigors of some dangerous mission or supersecret operation.

Back in college, when he'd walked out on her to join the army, she'd figured it was an empty threat. She had thought he'd come back, apologizing for blowing up at her, as he had so many times. But he hadn't. He'd not only joined the army, he'd qualified for the Special Forces division.

And now, looking at him, she knew he'd been captured or injured, and not long ago. He had not even recovered. She also knew he'd walked out again—this time from the hospital, against medical advice. She realized she was staring at him when he raised his gaze to meet hers. She blinked and looked down at her mug.

"So what are you going to do this morning?" he asked.

Suddenly the beautiful caramel color of the café au lait was about as appealing as mud. She pressed her knuckles against her mouth, hoping to quell the sobs building in her throat. Max was gone. Nothing else mattered. "I don't know," she said in a small voice.

Travis sent her an assessing look. "You need to go in to work," he said.

She immediately shook her head. "No. I couldn't concentrate. I couldn't talk to anyone without breaking down—" Her throat closed on the last word. She swallowed and blinked against the sudden haze in her eyes. She gestured toward her face. "See? Everybody would know that there is something very wrong with me."

"You've got a full schedule?" he asked.

She shook her head. "No. I cleared my schedule so I could prep for the trial. It starts in ten days and I haven't even finished reading the witness statements, much less interviewing the senator and whoever else I feel I need to talk to."

"Then that's what you should do. You go in and work on the trial. Isn't that what the kidnappers want you to do? You can't get your son back until the trial is done and it goes the way they want it to go. It would be good for you, make you feel like you're actually doing something to get him back. If you sit around here, you're just going to make yourself crazy."

Kate thought about it. What Travis said made a lot of sense. It was exactly something she'd have told a patient if the situations were reversed. But they weren't. She couldn't think like a shrink right now. She was thinking like a mother whose child was in deadly danger. "But—what if something happens? What if they call me?"

"You've got your cell phone—" He stopped, a thoughtful look on his face. "Your office number is published, right?" he asked.

She nodded. "Of course."

"What about your home number?"

"No. I don't like to publicize it or my cell."

"But the kidnapper called your cell, right?"

Kate thought about dropping the phone and having to scramble around to find the battery and the back. "How did they get my number?"

"Good question. Although I guess a lot of people have it."

Kate pressed her lips together. "Yes. Too many. I've probably been too lax with giving it out. It's just so much easier than trying to juggle the office and the home phones."

"So, are you going to go into work?"

"I don't—" She pushed her fingers through her hair. "I can't decide. All I can think about is Max."

Travis watched Kate. She'd always been the most levelheaded, together person he'd ever known. He'd loved that about her. His childhood had bordered on chaos, until his dad had suffered his first stroke. If his dad and mom weren't yelling at each other, one of them was yelling at the kids. And occasionally his older brother Lucas and Dad would get into it. Those fights were legendary—and terrifying to Harte and Cara Lynn, the two youngest. Travis had long ago appointed himself as their guardian, but he knew he hadn't been a good one. He'd always had too much of his dad inside him.

During the time they'd dated in college, Kate had taught him that life wasn't about bouncing from one argument to the next. She'd always represented quiet and security to him, until that night he'd finally pushed her too far.

Could he reverse the roles? Could he be her security for once? He had no idea. But at least he could try.

He put a hand on her shoulder. "Think about Max. That's good. Think about him and what you can do that will get him back to you the soonest."

"Work on the case," she muttered, and he could tell by her expression that she was considering the idea. "I should be working on proof that Stamps was temporarily insane when he shot Paul Guillame."

Travis smiled wryly. "That'll be a whole lot easier than you might think. Anyone who knows Paul knows that within about a half hour, he can make you feel one—" he held up a finger "—like you want to shoot him and two, like you're going insane."

"That could make it easy," she replied, a small smile lightening her face.

He squeezed her upper arm, his fingers savoring the delicate bones and the warm, firm skin. It was all he could do not to lean over and kiss that tiny, pretty bump right above the curve of her shoulder.

"But what about my secretary?" Kate asked, her brow creasing with worry. "She'll know something's wrong."

Travis took her hand. "Think about it, Kate. You trust her, right? With all the confidential information about your patients?"

She nodded. "Of course. She's the most discreet person I know."

"Maybe you *should* talk to her. She might be the perfect person to confide in. She'd never betray your secret, right?"

"That's right. Never."

"There you go. Why don't you get dressed and I'll clean up these dishes."

"It's still early. What about you?" she asked, trying to sound casual. "What are you doing today? Are you going to see your parents?" she asked.

"No. I don't want to see them right now. I came to see you."

Kate's heart thudded. She knew that. What she didn't know was why. So she asked him. "Why right now?"

He shrugged, his lean broad shoulders looking bony beneath the pullover shirt he wore. "I had some leave and I wanted—" He paused and took a breath. "For the past few months I've been thinking about you." He waved a hand impatiently. "It doesn't matter. We've got bigger things to worry about, like why it's so important to these people to get a temporary-insanity defense on this Stamps guy."

She wanted to make him talk about himself, about what had happened that had taken such a toll on him, physically and emotionally. But her fear for Max overrode her curiosity about Travis. If telling him everything she knew could get Max back, then she was happy to let him change the subject.

"Why didn't they just claim it was an accident?" he continued. "You said Paul was shot in some kind of a shoot-out? There must have been bullets flying everywhere."

"True, but from what Harte told me, Stamps threatened Paul right before all the shooting began, and despite what Paul claimed about being hit by a stray bullet, Stamps's gun was missing only one round." She turned to look at the clock on the stove. "It's seven-thirty. Do you think I should wait here until they call?"

"Until *who* call?" But as soon as the question left his lips, she could see that he knew the answer.

"The people who have my son," she said, letting impatience tinge her voice.

Kate felt panic rising in her chest. "Why don't they call? I have no way of reaching them. I've got nothing but that awful voice on the phone, telling me if I talk, he'll be gone forever. Oh, Travis, I am so scared," she said.

Travis stood and came around the counter. He pulled her into his arms. She laid her head against his shoulder for a brief moment. It was strange. She'd never liked being held when she was upset. It made her feel claustrophobic. But right now she thought that she could stay here forever, sheltered by Travis's strong arms. But of course she couldn't. Her child was missing, and being held in Travis's arms would not bring her one step closer to getting him back. She pulled away.

He shook his head as she stepped away from him.

"What?"

"You would never let me hold you when you were upset," he said, echoing her thoughts.

She almost smiled. "Maybe because I was always upset with you."

"Not always. Not now. You just don't like feeling out of control, and letting someone give you comfort or support was always an alien concept to you." He turned and walked over to the couch and sat down, then stood again and dug into the couch cushions. He came up with a red toy car made out of wood.

"So this is what was digging into my back all night," he said, looking down at it. He spun the wheels with a finger and watched until they slowed to a stop. There was an expression on his face that Kate had never seen before. The chiseled planes of his jaw and cheeks and chin were soft, as were his dark eyes. "I'm surprised I didn't dream I was back—" He stopped.

Kate stepped over and took the toy from him as casually as she could. She didn't want to act too interested in what he'd almost said. "Back where?" she asked.

He didn't answer.

She turned the car over and over in her hands. "This is Max's favorite toy. He likes to drive it up my arm and across my shoulders and down the other arm and down my leg and onto the floor—" Her throat closed.

"I had a car almost exactly like that when I was little," Travis said.

She didn't quite catch what he'd said. "What?"

"Come here and sit down," he said, sitting on the couch and patting the space beside him.

"I can't." She held the toy car to her chest and paced. "He's out there alone. He doesn't have any pull-up pants or juice or allergy medicine. What if they're not taking care of him? What if they haven't given him any food or taken him to the bathroom? Oh, dear God, I can't—"

"Come on, Kate. You've got to calm down. You're already exhausted and it's only been one day. Didn't you say the trial is what—ten days away? You have got to take care of yourself. It's not doing you or Max any good for you to worry yourself sick. Sit down here and tell me how it happened. Where was he? Where were you?"

She ignored his hand patting the couch cushion. "He was at day care. It was around four o'clock and I was getting ready to leave to pick him up. Right after I got the call telling me they'd taken him, the day care called. Their fire alarm had gone off and they'd smelled smoke. So they took all the children outside. But when they started back to the classrooms, nobody could find Max." She spread her hands. "How could they let those people take him?"

She turned and flung the wooden car against the wall.

"Hey, hey." Travis stood and pulled her to the couch. He urged her to sit, then sat beside her. "So the people who took him set off a fire alarm and grabbed him while the day-care workers were trying to keep up with a bunch of kids outside? What did the lady say when she called you?"

"She asked me if I'd picked Max up early."

"And what was your answer?"

Kate shrugged. "What could I say? I tried to act normal. I said I had picked him up. Travis, *they told me they'd kill him.*" Why did Travis keep asking her what she'd done? She'd done just exactly what they'd told her to do. She didn't dare do anything else. "The girl didn't even ask any questions. She was so relieved that he was all right." She laughed harshly.

"She believed you?"

"She'd have believed me if I'd told her he was picked up by aliens who were taking him to Disney World. That's how desperate she was."

Travis patted her hand. For some reason the inane gesture was comforting. She relaxed a little.

"Tell me about Max. How old is he? Don't you have some pictures?"

Kate stiffened, any semblance of relaxation swept away by his words. "He's four. And, sure, I suppose there are pictures around here somewhere."

He looked at her oddly. "You suppose?"

She shrugged, trying to think of something to say to take that odd, suspicious look off his face. Even Travis knew that a mother would have photos of her children everywhere. A part of her wanted to distract him, to stop this train of thought, but she had no idea how. So she sat there, her feet riveted to the floor. Would it make a difference if he knew? Would he be more—or less—inclined to help her?

She had no idea what the man—or boy— she'd known back in college, the enraged, scary boy who'd stormed out of her apartment and her life at the mere mention of marriage, would do. He'd been furious when she'd brought it up. He hadn't given her even a moment to explain. She knew how badly she'd handled that conversation.

She should have started by telling him she thought she was pregnant, instead of leading with the idea of getting married. She'd known how he felt about marriage. He'd talked enough about how miserable his parents were. But she'd been so nervous and she'd blurted the first thing she could think of to say, and he'd yelled and stormed out.

It wasn't until a week later that she'd discovered she wasn't pregnant after all. If she'd only waited. If only she hadn't mentioned marriage.

She waited now, wondering how he'd handle what he was destined to find out and berating herself for being a coward for not just telling him outright.

Travis stood and glanced around the living room. Kate cringed internally. The newest portrait she'd just had made was at the framers, but there was a scrapbook in the bookcase filled with photos of Max, and her bedroom was filled with framed snapshots of him.

Travis stood still, his gaze sweeping the area, then he stepped over to the shelf beside the television. Kate squeezed her eyes shut. Travis picked up the packet, shot her a glance, then lifted the flap and pulled out one.

For a long moment, he stood staring at it. Kate saw in her mind's eye what he was seeing. She'd worn a red dress and she'd dressed Max in a red plaid shirt with a little red bow tie. The portrait was beautiful. But the most interesting thing about it was how much Max looked like his dad. He had the same dark eyes, the same slightly wavy hair, the same long dark lashes.

Travis raised his head and pinned her with

his gaze. He held up the photo. It trembled in his hand. His face was drained of color except for two pink spots that stood out in his cheeks. His eyes were penetrating. If they'd been laser beams, she'd be cut in half.

"Kate?" he said, walking over and standing over her where she sat on the couch. He held up one of the photos. "When were you going to tell me that Max is my son?"

Chapter Four

"He is my son, isn't he?" Despite the certainty in his voice, Kate could see the doubt, the questions, in his eyes.

"He is," she said, her psychiatrist's brain noting the defensiveness in her tone. She cleared her throat and tried to make herself talk—and think—rationally, like a physician, not like a single mom finally confronting the father of her child—his child—who'd been abducted.

"God, Kate, why didn't you tell me?" His gaze dropped to the photo again. He stared at it for a long time.

"Tell you? Really?" she said, frustration and sarcasm winning out over rational discussion. She waited for him to answer his own question.

He pinched the bridge of his nose. "I know. You couldn't possibly know where I was. Hell, even if you had known, you wouldn't have been able to reach me." He looked up. "I thought you said he was four. It's been five years—"

She gave a little laugh. "You have to allow nine months for the pregnancy."

"Oh, yeah." He looked at the photo again, then slowly, he touched the front of it with a trembling finger.

He must have felt her watching him because he turned back toward the shelf and set the packet of photos down. He started to place the snapshot he held on top of the packet, then changed his mind. He cocked his hip in a familiar way that always set her heart to racing and her insides to thrumming. Sliding his wallet out of his hip pocket, he slid the little three-by-five photo into it, then returned it to his pocket.

A lump grew in her throat and she felt the threat of tears swelling behind it. He'd put the photo of his son in his wallet—because he wanted to be close to his son or because that photo might be the closest he'd ever be to him? "I should get ready to go to work," she said tightly, pushing the thought that Travis might never meet Max out of her mind. She'd never make it if she let thoughts like that in.

Travis turned to her and smiled. "You should. It'll be good," he said. "Trust me. You'll see when you get there. You need to figure out how you're going to make a case for temporary insanity."

Temporary insanity. What if Stamps had shot Paul to stop him from saying whatever he'd been about to say, as Harte and Dani claimed?

"Kate?"

She blinked and realized that, for one moment, she'd gotten caught up in the case. "You're right," she said. "I've got to get to work. There's a lot to do before the trial starts. I need to interview Danielle Canto, and probably talk to Harte again. I need to find out just exactly what Stamps said and did before he pulled the trigger." She stood. "I should get dressed."

Travis watched her walk determinedly into her bedroom and close the door. She'd finally started thinking clearly about Stamps's insanity defense. That's what she needed to do. It was the only way she could ensure her son's safety. Travis's thoughts screeched to a halt. *Their son.*

"My son," he whispered. The words felt alien on his tongue, like a different language.

He'd never intended to have a child. That notion was ranked Number Two on Travis's Top Five Taboos, right behind Number One, getting married. But that Top Five was dwindling fast. Another item on his taboo list had been seeing Kate again. He laughed shortly. So much for Travis's Top Five.

He glanced toward Kate's bedroom. He

needed her out of the house—preferably without her cell phone. She'd asked him to promise he wouldn't tell anybody. But the only thing he'd agreed to was not calling any of his police-officer brothers or cousins.

When he heard the pipes creak, telling him she'd turned on the water in her bathroom, he looked around for her purse, hoping she hadn't taken it into her room with her. There it was on the corner of the kitchen counter. Feeling guilty as hell, he fished in it until he came up with her cell phone, and pocketed it. Now, if he could just keep her distracted until she left the house without it.

BENT PARKED HALF a block from Dr. Chalmet's house in the Garden District at a few minutes after eight o'clock in the morning. He lowered the driver's side window and felt along the door panel to be sure his magnetic car sign was still in place. It was one of his best ideas ever. The sign advertised ACME Realtors with a large graphic of a house, an eight-hundred number and a bogus web address. Few people gave him a second glance once they saw that sign. Bent knew it was impossible to read the letters and numbers from more than about fifty feet away, but the graphic of a simple, boxy house with its pitched roof was the universal symbol for real estate agent.

Satisfied that his cover was in place, Bent took in Dr. Chalmet's house. Her Accord was parked in the driveway, but a little hatchback with a Maryland license plate was at the curb. He made a note of the license number for later reference. Then he spent about half a minute debating whether to call his contact or to wait and see what happened. He decided to wait and see if the doctor kept to her routine and headed to her office between eight-fifteen and eight-thirty.

Sure enough, at around eight-fifteen Dr. Chalmet got into her car and headed toward her office. The other car stayed put. Bent stayed put, too. He wanted to see the owner. It could be a family member or a friend. Hell, it could be the kid's father, except that none of his research had turned up a father. With a license plate from a thousand miles away, the owner of the hatchback couldn't be a cop. But as his law-enforcement training as well as his fourteen years on the police force in Chicago kicked in, Bent's pulse slammed into high gear. Montgomery County, Maryland, was so close to Washington, D.C., it might as well be part of the city. And Washington, D.C., housed, among many other things, the FBI. The Feds, who were always interested in kidnappings, especially those involving children. But they didn't usually drive, certainly not a thousand miles. They preferred to fly in one of the FBI's private jets and rent cars on the ground.

Besides, he was pretty sure the shrink was smarter than that. But even if she wasn't, he sure as hell was. He was out of here if the FBI was involved. He'd never gotten mixed up with a federal case and he never intended to. His jobs were short and sweet and clean, these days. When he'd first lost his job and his pension for taking bribes, he'd accepted any job that came his way, including hits. But he didn't like them. He still had enough police officer inside him to be bothered by taking a life. So he'd quickly moved into kidnapping for ransom. So far, he hadn't had to harm anyone.

He wasn't planning on breaking that record now.

He pressed the button to lower the driver's side window. Taking his phone from his pocket, he set it on camera. Then he settled back in the car seat, wishing he could smoke a cigarette but not wanting to do anything that would attract attention to him. He sat there, holding the phone in position to take a picture, and waited.

At ten-thirty-three, a man came out of Dr. Chalmet's front door. He was pale, and his clothes looked a size or two too big. He stood straight and tall, but he walked slowly, as if he were ill or injured. Bent surreptitiously snapped a few pictures as the man glanced around the neighborhood. As the man's gaze turned toward Bent's car, he froze, remaining perfectly still until the man's eyes had traveled past him.

He breathed a sigh of relief. The guy hadn't noticed him. To identify him as a tail and not react would make him one of the coolest guys Bent had ever seen. Would an FBI agent have that kind of cool? Bent didn't think so.

The guy yawned, then made his way to the hatchback. Bent assessed him and decided that he wasn't carrying. Even wearing clothes a size too big, it would be hard to completely hide even a small handgun. So he wasn't FBI. Maybe he was the kid's father. His client didn't mention a man in the picture, but it wouldn't be the first time a client hadn't known or had neglected to tell him everything about the target's neighbors, friends and family.

As the non-FBI agent cranked the car and pulled away from the curb, Bent debated what to do. Did he tail the sickly civilian or catch up with Dr. Chalmet at her office and stick with her, his top priority? As the hatchback passed his parked car without a second glance and turned right onto the next street, Bent started his engine and took the left, headed toward Dr. Chalmet's office.

TRAVIS WAS GLAD he'd waited to call Dawson's office. If he'd made the call before he had left the house, he might not have seen the kidnapper. Travis had excellent peripheral vision, one of the many reasons he'd easily qualified for Special Forces. He spotted the dark sedan that was parked half a block down from Kate's house without ever looking at it directly. He saw the real estate sign on the side, too, but he didn't believe it for a second. For one thing, there were no For Sale signs in the neighborhood. But he rarely made assumptions based on appearances. That kind of carelessness could be fatal on dangerous missions.

After yawning and making a subtle but obvious point of checking his pockets for the house key Kate had handed him as she'd left, he locked the door to the house, walked to his car and pulled away from the curb. As he passed the car, he noticed the sticker on the windshield. Then, after he had put some distance between them, he glanced in his rearview mirror without moving his head. The sedan's license plate was obscured with mud and dust, but he could read the first two numbers and the last. What he couldn't make out was the state.

Travis committed the numbers to memory. He would have liked to get a look at the driver, the man he was certain was Max's kidnapper, but he didn't want the man to know he'd made him.

Once he was sure the man was not following him, he dialed the number on an old card he had in his wallet, hoping Dawson's office number was still the same.

"Hello?" a woman's voice said.

"I need to speak with Dawson," Travis said.

"Dawson?" Her voice was carefully neutral. Travis knew that Dawson's investigations firm was exclusive. He didn't advertise and he rarely gave out his business cards. He liked his referrals by word of mouth. He didn't operate as Dawson Delancey for several reasons. He used John Dawson, his first and middle names.

"This is his cousin," Travis parried. She wasn't the only person who could be coy.

"Yes, and your name please?"

"Could you just tell him I'm here on leave? He'll know who I am."

"On leave? You're Travis?" the woman said. "Travis Delancey?"

Travis was shocked—and worried. He didn't recognize the voice, but then, he'd been gone five years, and it had been at least three years since he'd talked to any of his family. "Who is this?" he demanded.

"I'm Juliana Delancey. You don't know me."

Juliana Delancey? "No," he said, a question in his voice. "I don't."

"First, are you all right?" Her voice was crisp, yet tinged with worry.

"Yeah," he said. "Yeah, I'm all right. I've just got a situation I need to discuss with Dawson."

"Thank goodness," she said. "Unless I'm mistaken, it's been quite a long time since anyone has talked to you?"

Travis was getting more confused by the minute. "Who are you?" he asked again.

"I'm Dawson's wife, and partner in D&D Investigations."

For the second time, Travis felt as if someone had punched him. "Dawson's—what?" he stammered. From what he remembered about his cousin, Dawson had a longer taboo list than he did. And marriage was number one on his, as well.

"Yes," she said with a pleasant laugh. "It's wonderful to talk to you," she said. "You're the only one I haven't met. You said you're on leave. You're here, in New Orleans, right?"

Travis thought fast. "Listen—Juliana. I really need to get in touch with Dawson. But for the moment, I don't want anyone to know I called. It's kind of touchy and complicated, so—"

"Travis. Say no more. I understand. And as a

matter of fact, Dawson is in Chef Voleur today. He's helping his dad move some furniture."

"What?" Travis blurted again. More surprises. The last time Travis had been home, Dawson's feud with his father had been going strong.

"When's the last time you talked to your family?" she asked.

"About three years ago, before I was sent overseas."

"Then you've missed a lot. I'll give you Dawson's cell number. Give him a call. He was planning to be finished by noon or so. I'm sure you two can get together."

"Thanks," he said. At the next red light, he dialed the number she'd given him.

When his cousin answered the phone, he said, "Dawson, it's Travis. Don't say my name."

There was an almost imperceptible pause, then, "You okay?"

"Yeah. Can I see you today?"

"Sure," Dawson said without hesitation. "Hang on. Dad, I need to take this call. Be right back." Then a few seconds later, "Okay, I can talk now. What's up?" He sounded curious, but also crisp and professional, like his wife had.

Travis wanted to ask about Juliana and about Dawson's dad, but family stuff could wait. Kate's son—his son—was missing, and that was the most important thing right now. "I need your help, Dawson. Can we meet somewhere?"

"Where are you? Oh, you're calling on a New Orleans exchange. When did you get back?"

"Dawson, nobody can know I'm here. Not yet. I need to meet with you somewhere where nobody will know me. I need your help."

"Sure," Dawson said. "We've got an apartment in the French Quarter." He gave Travis the address and told him he could be there within an hour. "Depending on how traffic is on the causeway," he amended.

"How many Delanceys know about this apartment?" Travis asked.

"None," Dawson assured him. "Well, your brother Lucas did once, but he's probably forgotten all about it by now. He borrowed it from me when he first came back here from Dallas. And truthfully, it's not so much an apartment as it is a warehouse."

Travis was racking up the questions. He'd store this latest one—what was Lucas doing back in New Orleans when he swore he'd never return—with all the others until he had the luxury of time to catch up, which he didn't right now. "Should I wait in my car?" he asked.

"Nope," Dawson said. He gave Travis the combination to a mailbox on the outside of the building. "The key's inside the mailbox. Go to the fourth floor. It's the only door. Wait for me inside."

Travis drove to the address Dawson had given him and followed his instructions. He agreed with Dawson's assertion that *apartment* was not the right word for the large room that appeared to take up the entire top floor of the building. It had a bathroom and an alcove with a double bed that was separated from the rest of the room by a heavy curtain, and it was air-conditioned. The kitchen, however, consisted of nothing but a microwave and a mini-fridge on a countertop.

Travis turned on the AC and pulled a bottle of water out of the fridge. He sat down in a chair to wait for Dawson.

He'd barely finished the water when Kate's phone rang. The sound startled him and he dropped the plastic bottle. He cursed his damn jumpiness as he checked the display. The number was her office phone. He could picture her, fuming, ready to rip into him for sneaking her cell phone out of her purse. He hesitated, looking at the display, his finger hovering over the answer button. Then he shook his head. He didn't want to talk to her yet, and certainly not over the phone.

She'd probably get back to her house before he did, and find him gone. If she was fuming now, he didn't want to think about what she'd be like when he walked in tonight. He closed the phone. She'd have to wait. He needed to get Dawson on the trail of whoever had taken Max. That was the most important thing. He'd face her later. Hopefully he could show some results that would prove that he'd done the right thing in contacting Dawson. At the same instant that Kate's call went to voice mail, he heard footsteps on the stairs. There was a double rap on the door.

"Trav?" Dawson's voice came through the door. Then he heard a key turn in the lock and Dawson burst in, carrying a paper bag that he set on the bookcase just inside the door.

Travis couldn't help but grin when he saw his cousin. "Dawson," he said and stepped forward. The two men performed the basic man-hug—quick hand clasp and touch of shoulders, lightning-speed pat on back, then return to their corners. Dawson held on to Travis's hand for one extra split second, though, and assessed him. "You don't look so good, partner," he said, frowning. "What's the deal? Everything okay with you?"

Outside a car backfired. Travis jumped, then muttered a curse.

Dawson's assessing eyes narrowed. "Tell me what's up."

Travis gave his head a shake and his mouth quirked up in a smile. "How much time have you got?" he asked wryly.

"Actually, I've got all day. Dad and I had just finished moving the furniture when you called. I was going to run by and see Ryker, but hell, I see him and Reilly all the time. I haven't seen you in what? Three or four years?"

Travis nodded. "Yeah. And it sounds like a lot has happened while I've been gone. Apparently *you* found a ball and chain."

Dawson laughed, but Travis saw pride and contentment soften his face. It was an expression he'd never seen on his cousin's face—ever.

"Right," Dawson said. "What we need to be talking about right now is what's up with you. Let's sit down." He went over to the bookcase and retrieved the paper bag and brought it to the big oak table that sat near the windows. They each took a wooden hard-backed chair. Dawson pushed the paper bag toward Travis. "You still like café au lait?"

"Oh, man, thanks," Travis said, reaching inside the bag and pulling out a hot cup. He lifted the lid. "Sugar?" he asked.

Dawson got up and retrieved a mason jar half-full of sugar and a spoon from the counter where the microwave sat. "Juliana likes a lot of sugar, too."

Travis spooned sugar into the caramel-colored drink, stirred it vigorously, then took a long swig. "Mmm. There's nothing like real Louisiana chicory coffee."

Dawson took the other cup and sipped it. He didn't say anything else, just waited.

"What do y'all use this place for?" he asked.

Dawson shrugged. "A hideaway if we need to protect someone. We stay here if we have to be in New Orleans overnight. It's handy for lots of things. Jules wants to fix it up." Dawson shrugged and smiled.

Travis sent him an assessing look. Dawson married was a concept that was going to take some getting used to. Dawson drank his coffee in silence.

Finally, Travis took a deep breath. "I left Walter Reed AMA," he said.

Dawson nodded. "Against medical advice," he muttered.

"Yeah. I'd been on a mission—a long one." He shook his head. "I don't need to get into all that right now. Suffice it to say, I walked out, bought a car and drove down here."

"When was that?" Dawson asked, studying the plastic lid of his cup.

"I got here last night. Went to Kate's. Kate Chalmet is a psychiatrist. She—"

"I know her," Dawson said.

"You do?" Travis was a little surprised. Although he shouldn't have been, he supposed. Dawson worked as an independent investigator, but it made sense that he came into contact with the D.A.'s office and the people who worked there. Kate had already told him she had had dealings with his baby brother Harte, who was a prosecutor.

"Sure. She works for the D.A.'s office. Right now she's supposed to be making an assessment about whether Myron Stamps was insane when he shot Paul. Did you know he shot Paul Guillame?"

"Yeah, I heard," Travis said.

"So I'm guessing you weren't seeing Dr. Chalmet professionally?" Dawson looked up with a twinkle in his eye.

"Nope," Travis said. "She and I lived together for a long time while we were in college. It ended badly." He took a deep breath. "Look. I'll cut to the chase. Kate has a son—Max. He's four years old and he's—" To his dismay, Travis felt his voice catch. "He's mine," he said thickly, then swallowed hard.

Dawson's gaze went sharp. "Four years old?"

Travis nodded. "I came home on furlough five years ago and we—hooked up," he finished harshly. "I didn't know until this morning that Max is my son." He waved a hand. "So anyway, you know Kate is evaluating Stamps. I don't know the whole story but apparently it's in Stamps's best interest, or someone's, anyway, to be acquitted on grounds that he was temporarily insane when he pulled the trigger."

Dawson stayed quiet.

"Well, yesterday afternoon, somebody abducted Max."

Travis was surprised again when Dawson didn't react. But he supposed Dawson had heard it all.

"He disappeared from child care," he continued. "The child-care personnel were frantic, so they called Kate. She had just hung up from talking with the abductor. He had warned her that if she said anything to anybody, they'd kill her son—they'd kill Max." Travis cleared his throat. "She told them that she'd popped in and picked up Max without telling anybody. She said the girl who had called was so desperate to believe that Max was with his mom and okay that she had accepted Kate's explanation without question."

"When was that?"

"Around four o'clock yesterday afternoon. She hasn't heard anything since."

Dawson finished his coffee, then looked at Travis. "Did you tell anybody you were coming here?"

"What? Here?"

"New Orleans."

"No, I didn't. You think— No. Not a soul. Not even the used-car dealer."

"Okay, so the kidnapping is not about Delanceys. That's good. What can I do?"

Travis laid Kate's phone on the table. "This is Kate's phone. The phone the kidnapper called her on. I'm hoping you can trace where his call originated, or figure out where he bought the phone or something."

"Sure." Dawson reached for the phone.

"But first," Travis said. "There was a car outside Kate's house this morning. I can't say how long he'd been there. But he was there when she left for work, and he was still there, taking pictures with his phone, as I was getting into my car. He had a magnetic sign on the side of his car, advertising a real estate agency."

"Can you describe the car or the man?"

"I was trying to play it casual, so I couldn't get a good look at the man, and the license plate was obscured by mud. But I got the first two numbers and the last. Also, the sticker on the windshield was pretty distinctive. It had three stacked emblems on the left half, with two light blue stripes down either side."

"Good eyes," Dawson said.

"I was trained to notice everything and remember it."

Dawson nodded as Travis handed him a piece of paper where he'd written the car's make, model and what he'd seen of the license plate number. He'd sketched his description of the left half of the sticker.

"So he's from out of town. He's a pro."

"A pro?"

Dawson nodded as he tucked the note into his pocket. "A professional. They imported him. He must be awfully good at what he does. What did he do when you drove away?"

"He pulled out behind me, but he made a left when I turned right. Left is the way Kate goes to her office. I'm guessing that his instructions are to watch Kate. But he wanted to see who owned the Maryland car. Once he got a good look at me and took some pictures with his phone, I'm guessing he headed for Kate's office to keep watch on her."

"I've got a computer whiz who can do anything. I'll get Dusty on this as soon as I get back to the office. Now let's look at Kate's phone." Dawson picked up the phone and pressed a couple buttons, studying the display. He pressed another one, then another. Then he nodded and pocketed the phone. "I'll get Dusty started on this, too. We'll have some information soon. I don't know how much. What else?"

"How can I find Stamps? Do you know?"

"I know where his office is and Juliana can get his home address for you. Why?"

"I have to confront him and find out who took my son!"

"Hang on, Travis. It won't do you any good to go throwing your weight around. I'd hate for Stamps to hang a harassment charge—or worse—on you. Why don't I take care of it? I can send someone to watch his office and home, to see who comes and goes. Right now he's taking time off from his legislative duties, from what I understand, and is working with his attorney to prepare his defense in his upcoming trial."

Travis rubbed his face. "You can put somebody on him if you want to, but I'm still going to talk to him."

"I thought you didn't want anybody to know you're here. If you piss off Stamps, it's going to get around."

"It'll probably get around anyhow, since the Chicago guy took my picture, and it's a cinch he's reporting to someone Stamps knows if not to Stamps himself."

"What's the deal with hiding out from everybody? You haven't even talked to your mom?"

"No, and I'm not going to until I get all this sorted out." Travis heard his voice. He sounded stubborn, almost petulant.

Dawson assessed him for a moment. "So the only reason you checked yourself out of Walter Reed and drove all the way down here was to see Kate Chalmet? Did you want her to help you find a therapist here in town?"

"A therapist? What are you talking about?" Travis asked defensively.

Dawson shrugged. "It's pretty obvious, kid. You're suffering from PTSD."

Travis laughed, but not with amusement. "No, I'm not," he snapped, glaring at Dawson. "You think I need a shrink? I can assure you I don't."

"Hey." Dawson held his hands up. "I wasn't making a judgment. Just asking. So why'd you go to see her? You said you didn't know about the boy."

"That's right," Travis retorted. He grimaced, then unclenched his jaw. "Sorry," he said. "I'm just a little on edge right now." He sighed. "I went to see her because—" He stopped. He didn't speak for several moments. To his relief, Dawson sat quietly.

Finally Travis took a deep breath. He didn't want to talk about himself, but he figured if

Dawson was going to help him, he needed to know everything.

"I wasn't just on a long mission. I was captured," he said finally. "It's not important, got nothing to do with Kate and my—our—son. But the reason I drove straight to her house—" He stopped again.

Dawson picked up the tiny plastic triangle that he'd twisted off his coffee lid. He twirled it in his fingers, watching it.

"I was held captive for five months. It was beyond hell, and the only thing that kept me alive was thinking about the people I loved. My family—and Kate. Hell, Dawson. I don't want to talk about all that. I'll deal with it later. Now my priority is finding Max."

Dawson nodded and smiled. "Not a problem, Trav. I'll get right on it. Is that everything?" he asked.

"If you think it might help to tail Stamps, I'd like to know who all he sees and talks to."

"I'll put somebody on it."

"Just bill me," Travis said, and pushed back from the table.

"Hang on a minute. What do you know about Myron Stamps?"

"Me? Not a thing. Why?"

Dawson shook his head. "I'll fill you in so you'll know what you're dealing with. Myron

Stamps is a long-time state senator. He's probably only ten years younger than our granddad. You probably never heard him talk about the *Good Ole Boys,* did you?"

Travis shook his head. "Good old boys as in racist and bigoted with a pre–Civil War mentality?"

"Yeah, in general," Dawson acceded, smiling. "But specifically, the *Good Ole Boys* are a group of elder senators and congressmen who are following in the footsteps of Con Delancey. And Con, of course, patterned his entire political career after Huey Long. In their heyday, Long in the 1930s and Con in the sixties and seventies, they each courted the rural folks by such programs as Long's *Share the Wealth* and Con's *Work and Receive* initiative while pushing more and more power into the governor's hands and out of the legislature. Did you know Con ran for governor three times and lost? Grandmother was sure that he'd have been elected in 1990 if he hadn't been killed."

"I've heard some of those stories about Granddad. Not about him running for governor, though. What's all this got to do with Stamps?" Travis asked.

"Myron Stamps followed right along in Con's footsteps, only he and several other legislators who have been around for a long time called themselves the *Good Ole Boys*. These days there are only three left—Stamps, Darby Sills and Gavin Whitley. There have been rumors for years that they've taken bribes and kickbacks from businessmen in the import business to keep import taxes low and look the other way when certain illegal substances are brought in through the Port of New Orleans." Dawson took a drink of his coffee, then continued. "Danielle Canto overheard the men who had killed her grandfather yelling out Stamps's and Paul's names. The importer, Ernest Yeoman, was convicted of conspiracy to kill Freeman Canto. Your baby brother Harte was involved in the case."

Travis nodded. "Kate told me he was shot, but he's doing okay."

"Right," Dawson said. "So, like I said, Yeoman was found guilty of conspiracy, but Danielle Canto's testimony was the only evidence against Stamps or Paul, so they walked away. Stamps is on leave from the senate now, stating he's working with his attorney to prepare that temporary-insanity defense that the D.A. is bringing against him for shooting Paul."

"What's all this got to do with anything?"

"The other two *Good Ole Boys?* Sills and Whitley? They're still going strong. Still in office. Still advocating low tariffs. And they owe their careers to Stamps."

"Sills and Whitley." Travis frowned. "Are you saying they're somehow mixed up in all this?"

"Word is they'd do anything for Myron Stamps. So…" Dawson spread his hands, palms up.

Travis tried to wrap his brain around the concept that three state legislators would conspire to kidnap a child. "Kidnapping a child is a federal offense."

Dawson nodded.

"Why risk it? Stamps could plead down to simple assault."

"But that's still a felony. He couldn't hold public office."

"You said he's out of the senate?"

"Nope. Not out. Just taking a temporary leave of absence. If he manages to make this insanity plea stick, he could be back on the job within a year or two."

"That makes no sense. He's probably got the best attorney money can buy. From what Kate told me, Paul is not pressing charges. Why not plead innocent and claim it was an accident?"

Dawson shrugged. "I'm not saying it makes sense. I'm just trying to follow their logic—or illogic—tree. If he pleads not guilty and loses, he's out of politics for good."

Travis stood. "Okay," he said. "If you could put a man on Stamps, I'd appreciate it. But I'm still thinking about having a talk with him."

"He'll make you as a Delancey."

"Maybe that's not such a bad thing."

"Let me know what happens."

"I will," Travis said. "Listen, Dawson. Don't say anything to anybody about me being here."

"I won't, but I think you're making a mistake."

"I know. If it were me, I'd go to Lucas. But Kate believes the guy. He told her he'd kill Max if she told anybody. Any time I try to bring up going to one of my brothers or cousins who are on the job, she gets hysterical."

Dawson reached for the doorknob. "She was okay with you talking to me?"

At that moment the phone started ringing.

"Don't answer it," Travis said. "It's Kate. She knows I have her phone. She's called once already."

"This isn't Kate," Dawson said, holding up the phone so Travis could see the display. "It says *Private Number*."

"That's the kidnapper," Travis said.

Chapter Five

"Should I answer it?" Travis asked.

Dawson shook his head, then held up a finger as he clicked the speaker button with his other. "Hello," he said.

There was silence on the other end, then, "I told her what would happen if she told anybody."

"Who are you?" Dawson asked.

The man cursed.

"Don't hang up. I've got a deal for you."

Travis stared at Dawson, who nodded reassuringly at him, still holding up his hand.

Travis felt helpless, listening to Dawson dealing with the kidnapper while he stood there, having no idea what to do or say—or even think.

"A deal?" The voice laughed harshly. "Who the hell do you think you are?"

"I'm the guy who can get you what you want," Dawson said.

"I told Dr. Chalmet what I want."

"Right," Dawson drawled, cutting his eyes to Travis, who still wasn't sure what was going on. He just hoped Dawson knew what he was doing. "You want Senator Stamps to be ruled temporarily insane so he can skip out on his assault charge. That's what *you* want?"

"That's right," the voice said.

Travis realized that Dawson had taken control of the conversation. "No, it's not. What *you* want is money. It's the people who hired you that want Stamps off on an insanity plea."

"Same difference," the voice said petulantly. "What the hell is it to you? And hey. You still haven't told me who the hell you are."

"Nope. And I'm not going to. You don't need to know who I am. All you need to know is I've got plenty of money and I'm willing to give it to you to return Dr. Chalmet's son to her and walk away."

"How—" the voice stopped, then spoke again. "I took a job and I intend to finish it. But say you want to buy some insurance, be sure the kid stays healthy, that's fine with me. But I ain't walking out on a job. I got a reputation."

"Oh, you've got a *reputation*." Dawson hit the mute button, then looked at Travis. "Like I said, he's a pro."

"Hell, yeah, a good one," the man on the

phone said. "Now you'd better let me speak to the doctor, *now*."

"So he's a pro—a professional kidnapper?" The idea that his son was being held by a man who kidnapped children *for a living* horrified Travis.

Dawson shrugged and pressed his lips together. "My guess is he does more than just kidnappings."

Travis's stomach felt as if it had hit the floor. "You think he's a hit man," he said.

"He's not going to hurt the boy," Dawson responded quickly. "He needs him."

Although that was what Travis had told Kate to reassure her, Dawson's words didn't make him feel a whole lot better. He was becoming more and more worried about Max. Where was the man keeping him? Was he safe and warm? Was the man feeding him and giving him enough to drink?

Dawson held up his hand again and took the phone off Mute. "I'm representing Dr. Chalmet," he said into the phone. "You can talk to me."

"Oh, hell, no," the man said. "I don't talk to her right now, I'm hanging up and she can kiss her kid goodbye."

"You're not going to hurt the kid. He's your ace in the hole."

"Look, asshole. I heard the trial's been moved up. If the doctor doesn't know that already, you tell her," the kidnapper went on. "And tell her this. She missed her chance to talk to her kid. Little sucker's been whining so I thought maybe he'd like to hear his mama's voice. But that ain't happening now. I'll call back one more time and when I do, she better be there to talk to me or I'll hang up and hell will freeze over before she ever sees her kid again. You got that?"

Travis touched Dawson's arm and pointed to himself. Dawson shook his head.

"I got it. Dr. Chalmet will be very sorry she missed your call, but she's busy working on your demands. So there's no reason to punish her or her child because she's doing what you told her to. Why don't you call back at seven o'clock this evening and—"

There was a click on the line. The man had hung up.

"Damn it!" Travis cried. He whirled around and kicked the chair nearest him.

"Take it easy, Trav. That temper of yours won't do your son any good. I'd have thought Special Forces might have trained that out of you."

Travis instantly regretted the outburst. He was a little surprised at himself. He hadn't blown up like that since the first two weeks of boot camp. He'd thought—hell, he'd hoped and prayed—that the rage he'd always harbored inside him, like his own personal demon, was gone.

Chagrined, he walked over and picked up the chair. "I never had a son—" He stopped and swallowed, looking down at his white-knuckled fist doubled around the back of the chair.

Dawson's large hand squeezed Travis's shoulder for a second. "We'll get him back. I promise."

Travis's gaze snapped to Dawson's. "Don't say that if you don't mean it, Dawson. Especially not to Kate. She's fragile, barely holding it together. It hasn't even been twenty-four hours yet."

"And that's good. I'm glad you didn't wait to contact me. By the way, did you notice the man's accent?"

"He had an accent?"

"Definitely Midwestern. I think he may be from Chicago."

"That's pretty specific."

"Your brother Lucas's wife has a brother who lives up there. His kids are picking up the accent. That means Dusty can narrow the search field. The sooner we get on this—" he held up the phone "—the better. I need to get going. My computer whiz is in Biloxi. I can do a little, but the kid's a genius."

Travis nodded.

"I'm going to put that tail on Stamps, too. So if you go to see him, give me a call first. Put my number in your phone."

"I don't have a phone."

Dawson's brows shot up. "Don't have a phone? You've got to have a phone. Walk with me. I keep a few burner phones in my trunk, just in case. I'll give you a couple of them. Give one to Kate, to take the place of this one."

The two of them headed downstairs. When Dawson retrieved the phones and handed them to Travis, he looked at them and frowned. "How's Kate going to get calls from the kidnapper?"

"Oh, that's easy enough," Dawson said. "Hang on." He pulled Kate's phone out of his pocket. "Give me that phone." He pointed to one of the phones Travis held. He used his thumb to press buttons on it, looked at the display, then pressed buttons on Kate's phone. Glancing from one device to the other, he nodded. "Okay," he said. "Now any call that comes to Kate's phone will be forwarded to that phone. Explain that to Kate when you give it to her."

Travis nodded.

"As soon as I get back to the office, I'll get Dusty to fix it so that we can listen in on any calls. Tell Kate that, too. Tell her anything that is said on the phone will be recorded. Tell her to try and get as many specifics as she can out of the guy."

"That's great, Dawson. Thanks," Travis said. "I don't know how to—"

"Hey," Dawson said, grasping his shoulder briefly again. "Don't worry about it. Just keep me up to date on what's happening with the trial."

"Right. That guy said the trial date's been moved up. I'll bet that's why Kate called. I didn't answer the phone because I didn't want to listen to her yell at me for taking her phone and contacting you. She's going to be so mad at me." Travis ran a hand through his hair. "And I can't blame her. When she finds out the kidnapper called, she's going to panic."

"Tell her I recorded that whole conversation. And tell her not to worry. He's not going to hurt your boy. He's going to call back at seven o'clock and he's going to let Kate talk to him."

"How can you be sure of that?"

"Because I told him to. The guy's a pro. He's got sense enough to keep her as calm as possible. If she's too distraught, she won't be able to do her job. That's why I was careful to remind him that she wasn't available to talk to him because she's working on the case."

Travis nodded again. "I couldn't have done this on my own, Dawson."

"Hey, kid, you've got a whole different set of skills. When you confront this kidnapper, you can take him down and beat the crap out of him."

Travis was a little taken aback. "That's not how we work," he said.

Dawson's eyes narrowed assessingly. "Sorry. I guess I still see you as a pissed-off kid, instead of a Special Forces operative. No offense."

Travis held out his hand. "Thanks."

Dawson took his hand and the two of them man-hugged again.

Then Travis looked up and down the street. "I better get going. If the town is like I remember it, someone we know will walk up before long."

Dawson smiled. "It's not easy being the grandkids of the most infamous politician in the state."

"You got that right." Travis headed toward his car.

Dawson opened his car door, then called out to Travis. "Kid," he said. "I'll call you after the kidnapper calls."

"What if he doesn't call?"

Dawson tipped an imaginary hat. "He'll call."

TRAVIS DROVE TO Myron Stamps's home in Metairie. It was a large two-story house with white pillars. There was a brick fence across the front of the property with urns in the place of lions sitting on top of the concrete posts that flanked the driveway. Travis drove straight in and parked the bedraggled little hatchback next to a Lexus that was so dark green it could have been mistaken for black.

When he rang the front doorbell, Stamps himself answered. He was a small round man with thinning hair. He had on a polo shirt and pale green slacks. "You're early—" he started to say as he swung the large door open. "Oh."

"You're Stamps?" Travis asked pointedly.

"I'm Senator Stamps," he said, peering questioningly at Travis. "Who are you?"

Travis eyed Stamps's clothes. "Going golfing?" he guessed.

Stamps stepped backward and started to close the door.

"This won't take long," Travis said, putting out an arm to stop the door. "I have some questions for you."

"Wait a minute," Stamps said. "I know who you are. You're a Delancey."

"Good job," Travis said, then pushed past him and walked into the marble-floored foyer. "Nice," he drawled, turning around to face Stamps, who was staring at him in mild shock.

"You can't just walk into my home uninvited. If you don't leave immediately, I'll call the police."

"No problem," Travis said, smiling at the senator. His expression seemed to startle the man. "You can call Lucas, Ethan, Ryker or Reilly. There's also Shel Rossi, who's a cousin of ours. And—" he snapped his fingers "—you know, if you wanted to call a judge, you could give Shel's dad, Judge Rossi, a ring. He's my uncle."

"What the hell do you want, Delancey? Which one are you, anyhow?"

"That has nothing to do with why I'm here. But what I want? Well, that's what we're about to talk about."

Stamps took a couple phlegmy breaths as he studied Travis. He tucked his polo shirt a little more snugly over his belly and into his green pants, then he gestured toward the right.

If Travis weren't mistaken, there seemed to be a small flicker of fear in the senator's eyes

as he said, "You might as well come in. No
sense in standing in the foyer." He pronounced
it *foy-yay*.

Travis headed in the direction Stamps was
pointing and stepped into a darkly paneled
room. Behind him, Stamps turned on the lights.
It was the very cliché of a study. Deep red carpeting and curtains, mahogany desk, leather
executive's chair, three club chairs and each
wall lined with bookshelves.

"This is nice, too," Travis said, gesturing to
the dark leather and wood around him. "Never
knew working for the government was so lu-
crative."

"Your granddaddy did all right," Stamps
muttered, going behind the desk and sitting. He
pulled the curtains, exposing French doors that
opened onto a patio. Then he turned and picked
up a letter opener that seemed to be a tiny rep-
lica of General Lee's ceremonial sword, complete with tassels, and fiddled with it. "Why
don't you have a seat and tell me what you
think I can do for you?"

Travis didn't sit. Instead he propped a hip
on Stamps's desk. Then he leaned down until
his face and Stamps's were no more than six
inches apart. "I'll tell you what you can do for
me, *Senator*."

"Wha—" Stamps pushed his chair back. "I told you to sit down."

"You listen to me, old man," Travis growled. "I don't know what you think you're doing threatening Dr. Chalmet, but you'd better back off or I will personally put you in the hospital."

Stamps stared up at Travis, seemingly horrified. "You'd better watch yourself. You're threatening an elected official. That's a federal crime."

"I'll tell you what's a federal crime. Kidnapping a child. Now, *that's* a federal crime with some serious teeth behind it." He stood up and walked back around the front of the desk and sat in one of the club chairs. "Unlike, as you put it, *threatening* a washed-up senator who hasn't got a prayer of getting out of court without a felony conviction."

Stamps pulled a white handkerchief out of his coat pocket and wiped his face. Then he stood and rested his knuckles on the top of the desk. "I have no idea what you are talking about. What child? What threats? And who is Dr.—did you say Chalmet?"

"I'm sure you're keeping all that well away from yourself. Who's doing the dirty work? Is it Senator Darby Sills? The one with all the money? No." Travis put his fingers to his chin as if he was thinking very hard. "No. It's probably Congressman Whitley. He's your newest recruit into the *Good Ole Boys,* isn't he? Probably getting harder to find your kind of politician these days, isn't it? Poor Whitley—having to perform your dirty little tricks."

"I still have no idea what you're talking about, Delancey. Now I'd suggest you get out of here. I do know a couple police officials who are not Delanceys." Stamps reached for his desk phone.

Travis caught the senator's wrist. His middle and ring fingers pressed the back of the wrist, his thumb was positioned right in the center of the front. "You want me to demonstrate my skills for you, Myron?" He applied pressure with his thumb, enough to force the senator's fingers to curl. "I can break your wrist without straining an eyebrow hair. Want to see?"

Stamps started to pull against Travis's grip.

"Careful," Travis warned. "You probably should stay still. If you break your own wrist by moving like that, I can't be responsible for the integrity of the bones. They might shatter and you'd never be able to use that hand again. I, on the other hand, know how to break it cleanly. No shattered bones."

Stamps's ruddy face turned a sickly pale purple color. "I demand that you let me go," he croaked.

"I will, as soon as you tell me who set up the kidnapping."

"I told you I—"

Travis moved his forefinger and thumb slightly.

"Aah!" Stamps cried. "Oh my word, oh my word. You broke it."

"No. I just touched a nerve. Want me to do it again?"

"No!" Stamps bent over the desk in the direction of his hand, obviously hoping to take any strain off the bones. He was terrified that Travis's hold would shatter his wrist. "I swear I don't know what you're talking about."

"Not a good answer." Travis glanced toward Stamps's hand.

"No, wait. Please." Stamps cleared his throat. Sweat trickled down his temple and ran into the creases of his jowls. "The only one who would do something that stupid is Whitley," he mumbled.

"Whitley can't be doing this alone," Travis growled. "He doesn't have the money to hire a pro. Is Sills paying for it, or are you?"

"I'm not! I swear."

Travis groaned exaggeratedly. "My fingers

are getting tired. When they get too tired, they start twitching. If they twitch in the wrong direction—"

Stamps's mouth dropped open. He looked dumbfounded. "No—" he breathed.

Travis watched him, thinking if the senator was acting, he was doing a damn good job of it. Could he be telling the truth? Could the whole kidnapping have been dreamed up by Sills or Whitley, or both of them together? "No, what?" Travis asked, scowling at Stamps.

"They *kidnapped* somebody?" Stamps swallowed audibly, then coughed.

"Not just somebody. A child. A four-year-old boy," Travis said.

What little color had been in Stamps's face drained away pale. "I didn't know."

Travis studied Stamps closely. His face was still that light purple color. His lips were pinched and white at the corners. And his face and neck were dripping with sweat. His eyes were dilated, and through his fingers on the man's wrist, Travis could feel his pulse, which was fast and shallow. The man had been a politician for fifty years, so Travis doubted he'd be this shaken if he were lying.

On the other hand, Travis had seen men react this way when threatened with death. Stamps might be a scumbag. He'd probably shot cousin Paul on purpose. But Travis didn't think Stamps had known about the kidnapper.

He glanced at his watch. "It's about three minutes to four. Your golfing buddy is probably here. Who is he?"

"It's—" Stamps shook his head, as if trying to clear it. "It's the mayor. We're just—just going to work on our putts on my p-putting green for an hour, then head to a dinner meeting."

"That sounds like fun. Your buddies Sills and Whitley going to that meeting?"

Stamps shook his head so hard his jowls shook. "No. I mean, I don't know. This is a community thing. Not political at all."

Travis squeezed gently with his thumb.

Stamps gasped and winced.

Travis smiled, but the senator didn't look mollified. "Let's not mention my visit, okay? Let's keep this just between us. And remember, I might come to see you again if I don't find out what I need from your buddies." He let go of Stamps's hand and the man rubbed it as if he'd had on tight handcuffs.

"By the way, where would I find your two buddies this afternoon? Do you have any idea?"

Stamps shook his head again. "I—I think Whitley is in Baton Rouge. But Sills? You—

you can c-call my secretary. She'll track him down for you." He gave Travis the number.

Travis stored it in his phone, pocketed it, then pointed at Stamps's wrist. The senator stepped backward. "Remember," Travis said. "Just between us. Got it?" he asked, smiling.

Stamps nodded, sending his jowls quivering in an entirely new direction.

Chapter Six

Travis got to Kate's house at fourteen minutes until seven. He'd called Stamps's secretary and found out that Darby Sills was scheduled to attend the same dinner Stamps and the mayor were attending. He wasn't above confronting the senior senator there, but by the time he found out where Sills was, it was after five-thirty and he was facing driving across the Lake Pontchartrain Causeway during rush hour. Just as he'd figured, it had taken over an hour to get back to Kate's house.

He breathed a sigh of relief as he closed the front door behind him. Then he saw Kate. At the same time, she saw him and cried his name. She was barefoot and she'd obviously been pacing the living room.

He met her gaze as her expression, frantic with fear, turned to anger and her pale cheeks flushed. Then the anger morphed into a cold stare that could have flash-frozen hot coffee. "Give me my phone," she snapped.

"Kate, listen to me. We don't have much time."

"Give—me—my—phone. How dare you take it from me?"

He took a deep breath. "I don't have your phone," he said quietly. He rose to the balls of his feet, bracing himself for her to explode, fully expecting her to come flying at him with her fists doubled. But she surprised him.

She stood perfectly still, her back ramrod straight, her expression eerily calm and composed. But Travis saw the tracks of tears on her cheeks. More than that, he saw the brittle tension that was holding her together. One tiny crack in that fragile facade and she would shatter. Sadly, he knew that his next words would be like a sledgehammer to her very frail shell of calm.

"I left it with my cousin Dawson." He held up his hands, palms out. "He's not a cop. He's a private investigator."

Her expression didn't change, but her face turned pale and her hand fluttered to her chest. "Your—cousin?" she said, swaying slightly. "Why did you do that? You promised me."

Travis watched her carefully. Was she going to faint? He stepped close to her and placed a hand on her elbow. She went rigid at his touch. "I'm going to explain. Okay?"

She didn't answer, but she let him lead her to the couch and urge her to sit. He sat beside her. Her gaze was so full of betrayal and desperate fear that it made his heart hurt.

"I didn't go to the police," he said. "I promised you I wouldn't."

She looked at him for a long moment, then down at her hands. "Now I can't talk to the kidnapper. He's going to hurt Max."

Travis reached for her hands but she clenched them together in her lap. "It's okay," he said. "Dawson's got a computer guy that can hack into your phone. He's going to trace the kidnapper's call. Figure out where the signal originated, where the guy bought it—everything he can."

"He'll know, the kidnapper will know—and then he'll—" Her breath caught on a sob.

"No, hon. No. He probably won't find out, but even if he does—he's not going to hurt Max. Dawson said the same thing I did. These people need Max. He's the only hold they have over you. If something happens to him, they'll have nothing. They've got to keep him safe and healthy."

"But—"

Travis put a finger against her lips. "Shh. Let me tell you what Dawson said."

She turned her head away from his fingertip and clenched her hands in her lap again.

Travis hated what he was doing to her. He'd known that going to Dawson was a good idea. He'd also known it would be difficult to explain it to Kate. But this was harder than he'd expected. The bewildered, betrayed expression on her face nearly broke his heart. He could only pray that he'd done the right thing.

"Dawson gave me a phone for you to use. As soon as he finished talking with the kidnapper, he programmed your phone to forward all calls to this one." Travis reached into his pocket and retrieved the burner phone.

Kate reached for the small black device. Travis gave it to her and she held on to it with both hands, as if she were afraid it would disappear.

"So any calls you receive—" he continued.

"Will transfer to this one?"

"That's right," he said, relieved that she wasn't too distraught to understand. He smiled at her.

But suddenly, her eyes grew wide and her face went completely white. "You said— Oh my God!" Kate's hand went to her mouth. "Your cousin—he talked to the kidnapper?

What did he say? What did he do? Is Max all right?" Tears sprang to her eyes.

Travis caught her hands. "Listen to me, hon. I know you're scared. I am, too. But Dawson knew just exactly how to handle him. The kidnapper's going to call back—" he glanced at his watch "—any minute now. The call will come through this phone. We think he's going to let you talk to Max."

"Talk to Max?" Kate's ravaged expression brightened a little. "Really? I can talk to him?"

And then he watched helplessly as she crumbled like one of those buildings that implodes in on itself.

She collapsed against the couch cushions, covered her face with her hands and cried. This wasn't a stoic, silent weeping, characterized only by the tears that coursed down her face. This was a full-on breakdown, with heart-wrenching sobs that seemed to be torn from her soul.

Travis fell mute. He'd feared she would break down, but this was more awful than he'd imagined. There was nothing to do but offer his comfort. He put his arm around her tentatively, giving her the choice of rejecting or accepting his embrace. She stiffened. But he remained still, barely touching her, giving her the option of pulling away. Finally, she leaned into him, burying her face in the hollow between his neck and shoulder, her delicate back shaking, her tears soaking his shirt.

He held her and murmured meaningless words. He wasn't sure what all he said. Meaningless things like *it's going to be okay,* and *don't worry, everything's going to be all right.* He didn't know where he'd learned how to comfort, but he remembered holding Harte and Cara Lynn and whispering to them while their dad had shouted and cursed at their mother or Lucas.

It seemed like a long time later when Kate finally stopped sobbing and merely sniffled occasionally. Her breath cooled his tear-soaked shirt. As she quieted, he turned his face toward her hair and breathed in the strawberry scent that he remembered. She still used the same shampoo.

Lifting his arm carefully so as not to startle her, Travis looked at his watch again. Four minutes after seven. Why hadn't the kidnapper called? He blew out a frustrated breath.

Kate stirred, then pulled away. When she lifted her head, her face was splotchy and tear-streaked. She blinked, then looked at him wide-eyed, her wet, matted lashes surrounding her blue-green eyes like dark starbursts. "What's wrong?" she asked, and sniffled.

"Nothing," he said automatically.

She narrowed her gaze. "Yes. Something's wrong." She scowled. "You said the man would call any minute." Her breath hitched. "He's— Oh, God, he should have called by now. He's not going to, is he?"

"He's only a couple minutes late," he murmured as he pushed a damp strand of hair away from her cheek and brushed it back at her temple. Then he looked solemnly into her eyes. "Listen to me. Dawson's going to be recording every word both of you say. You need to get the guy to talk, to be as specific as possible about what he's doing and why."

Kate's tongue slipped out to moisten her lips and Travis's body, to his disgust and dismay, reacted immediately. After holding her close for those long moments, he was so in tune with her, so filled with the sight and scent and feel of her, that he was already half turned on. Now the sight of her tongue stirred him and made him long to taste it and the inside of her mouth. To kiss her and feel her kissing him back, like they'd done in college, when they were still in love.

But this wasn't the time. Hell, it might never be the right time for that again. This was about Kate and her son, and his attempts to help her get her little boy back. It wasn't about anything else. Certainly nothing to do with him.

He pulled her closer, willing to do nothing but hold her as long as she needed holding. But she kept her gaze on his for a second, then, to his surprise, she looked at his lips. He swallowed.

"Travis," she said softly, her eyes glittering with dampness.

"I know," he said. "I'm here. I'll be here as long as you need me."

She brought a hand up and touched his neck, then pressed her lips to the place she'd touched, the place where his pulse hammered.

He closed his eyes. He'd never in his life felt anything softer and sweeter than her lips on him. Even now, just that soft brush of skin against skin. Nothing more than Kate's attempt to make a connection with another person when she was missing her child so desperately.

But her lips stayed there, at his pulse point, then they slid up to his jaw and farther, until she could reach no higher. He bent his head, still passive, still not presuming that she actually wanted to kiss him.

A small moan of distress—or longing—escaped her lips and her hand, pressed against his chest, clenched around the material of his shirt.

The phone rang.

Kate jumped at the harsh jangle. For an instant, she didn't realize she had grabbed a fistful of his shirt. His arm tightened briefly around her shoulders. He bent his head and touched his forehead to hers.

"That's him," he whispered. "Go ahead, you'll do great."

She turned her head toward the phone, sitting on the coffee table. As she reached for it, the ringer jangled again, and she had the impression that it moved. She stared at the display that read *Private Number.*

Travis touched her shoulder and nodded at her. "Get specifics," he whispered. "And try to take control of the conversation."

Kate leaned forward and picked up the phone with a shaking hand. She had no idea what she was going to say. No idea whether she could talk. Her throat was quivering. She pressed her hand against it. She had to stay calm. All she wanted to do was talk to Max. But she had to talk to the kidnapper first, and she was not going to let him hear her crying.

"Max needs you to be calm," Travis muttered in her ear as she pressed the answer button with her finger. For some reason, his words helped.

"Hello," she said.

"Dr. Chalmet, it's good to finally hear *your*

voice," the man drawled. "A man answered your phone earlier. Didn't I tell you not to tell anybody?"

His voice was low and threatening. Kate had an overwhelming urge to beg him to forgive her and please not hurt her baby, but Travis had warned her to take control of the conversation, so she did her best to picture the man as one of her patients, a delusional schizophrenic.

"I want to speak to my son," she said as firmly as she could. Beside her, Travis leaned in to listen, his hand still on her shoulder, squeezing gently.

"You don't get to say what you want, Doctor. I'm in charge, and I'll let you know when you can talk to him."

A lump rose in Kate's throat. She didn't think she could live another second without hearing her baby's voice. She swallowed against the lump and took a fortifying breath.

"I want to talk to him now!" she said in her *doctor-in-charge* voice. It didn't sound quite as commanding as she'd hoped it would. She wondered how much of her desperate fear the man could detect.

"Shut the hell up and listen to me," the man yelled. "Do you think I care about what you want? Well, I don't. We need to talk business. Then, if you're good, *maybe* I'll be generous.

But only if you keep your mouth shut and listen to me."

Next to her, Travis put his finger to his lips.

She nodded. "Okay," she said into the phone. She took a deep breath and pressed her knuckles against her teeth for a brief instant. "Okay."

"Good. It always helps to have a sensible parent."

Always helps? "You've kidnapped children before," she whispered.

A brief pause told her that he hadn't meant to reveal that. "That's right, Doctor. Very good. I'm a professional. So be very clear—I know what I'm doing."

"Do you think that makes me feel better?" Kate said. "Do you think I'm *happy* that you've got lots of experience with abducting children and torturing their parents?"

"To tell you the truth, Doc, I don't think anything about you. I don't *care* about you. All I care about is getting the job done that I was hired to do. Now I need you to listen…to…me! Do you understand?"

"Yes, I understand."

"Now." The man took a long breath and let it out. "The trial date has been moved up—"

"What?" Kate vaulted to her feet. "When? When did that happen? Nobody told me anything about—"

"Shut! Up!"

Travis stood beside her, but she waved him off. "I'm okay," she mouthed silently. She wasn't okay, not by a long shot. But the more she interrupted, the more she protested, the longer it would be before she could speak to Max. And if she made the man angry enough, he might hang up without letting her talk to her little boy at all.

"The trial date has been moved up to Monday," he said. "That's only five days from now. Are you ready?"

Five days from now. That meant if she did everything that this awful man wanted her to, she'd be able to get her son back five days sooner than she'd thought. "No," she said, as calmly and professionally as she could. "I'm not ready yet. I haven't finished going through the case file. And I need to talk to Senator Stamps and the witnesses."

"Come on, Doc. How hard is it to stipulate that he was temporarily insane when he shot that guy? You don't need to read all the witness statements and reports. You sure don't have to talk to them."

Kate frowned at Travis. The man sounded like an attorney. Or maybe someone in law enforcement. He was comfortable with the correct terminology.

"I like to have all the facts before I present my findings," she said.

"That's admirable. But really, is there any question about what your findings are going to be in this case? After all, if you testify that Stamps was sane, then we no longer have an agreement, right?"

A stabbing pain caught Kate in the pit of her stomach. She gasped. "Please," she said pitifully, then caught herself. She took a long breath. "If I don't show that I've evaluated Senator Stamps and the situation thoroughly, I could be reversed on appeal."

The man laughed. "I know that, Doc. But I don't give a crap about appeals. You swing the temporary-insanity plea and I'm outta here. Look. I don't have a dog in this fight. I'm doing what I was hired to do. Now I'm suggesting you do what I've told you. And you're going to have to do it faster, because the trial date's been moved up. What you're going to do hasn't changed, now, has it?"

"No," she said. "It hasn't changed."

"Now I'll call you again, and when I do, your phone better not be in someone else's hands. Is that clear?"

"Yes," she said, her breath hitching with rising panic. *Don't hang up,* she begged silently. "Yes, it's clear." Dear God, she wanted to ask him, to beg him, to let her speak to Max. But he'd already warned her once. She held her breath, waiting to see what he was going to do.

She heard a soft scraping sound, as if he'd put a finger over the speaker, then nothing but silence. It went on for so long that she looked at the display, afraid that he'd hung up. But just as she put the phone back to her ear, she heard a woman's voice, far away, as if she were in another room.

"Settle down. I'm coming," the woman said, then, "Come on, honey."

Max. Kate's heart squeezed so tightly in her chest that she thought she might pass out. She felt Travis's hands on her upper arms. He guided her back to the couch and she sat. She switched the phone to her left hand. The right one was cramping from holding it so tightly.

"Max?" she breathed.

"Okay," she heard the man say, holding the phone away from his mouth. "Just a couple seconds. Got it?"

"Yeah, yeah," the woman said irritably. "Honey," she said tenderly, "say hi to Mama, okay?"

"Mommy?"

The small, anxious voice took Kate's breath away. She put her hand over her mouth to stop the sobs that escaped her throat. "Ma-ax?" she stammered, then held the phone against her chest, trying to muffle the speaker so her baby wouldn't hear her cry.

"Mah-mee?" Max's whine, muffled by her blouse, ripped through her like a razor blade.

"Oh—" she wailed, every inch of her body aching with the pain of being separated from her child. She squeezed her eyes shut. Travis took her right hand in his and held it to his chest. She could feel his heart beating through his skin, through his ribs, through the flesh of his hand that surrounded hers. She didn't know how he did it, but just the rhythm of his heart and the warmth of his hand gave her strength.

She lifted the phone to her ear. "Max, hi," she said, as calmly as she could. She didn't open her eyes, but she did force a smile, hoping it would come through in her voice. "Hi, honey."

"Mah-mee? Where are you? Come get me. I wanna go home."

"Maxie, honey, I know. You'll be—" She held her breath, trying to stop the sobs. Travis's hand squeezed hers. "You'll be home real soon."

"I don't like this place," he said. "They don't got movies. I wish I had my car."

"I know, sweetheart. It won't be long. Don't you have any toys there?"

"Yeah," he said. "I mean, yes, ma'am."

Kate smiled through her tears. He was just learning how to say yes and no ma'am. She clutched at her chest. Oh, she felt so empty without him. "What kind? Good ones?"

"There's a bear and a big choo-choo train, and some books."

"That's great. Can you read the books? Do you remember the words I showed you?"

"That's enough," Kate heard the kidnapper say.

She crushed the material of her blouse in her fist. "Max? Maxie, honey?"

"Mommy? Mahhh-meeee!" he cried suddenly, bursting into tears. "Mahhhmeeee-hee-hee?"

"Get him outta here!" the kidnapper growled. He'd taken the phone away from Max.

Kate heard Max crying and screaming "Mommy" as he was carried back to wherever they were keeping him.

"You bast—"

"Watch out, Doc, if you know what's good for you and your son. I mean it."

Kate did her best to compose herself. She sucked in a harsh breath and spoke crisply. "You have to tell me that you're taking care of him. Is he getting enough to ea-eat? Is that woman staying with him all the time?" The more questions she asked, the calmer she became. There *was* someone there taking care of her child. Max had actually sounded fine. He hadn't started crying until the man took the phone away from his ear.

"You just do what you're told and your kid'll be fine."

Kate blotted tears from her cheeks. "I'm trying to. Just please tell me—" She heard a click, and the line went dead. She turned to Travis. "He hung up," she said, holding out the phone.

Travis took it from her and looked at the display, then set it on the coffee table and held out his arms. Kate didn't hesitate. She went to him.

He wrapped his arms around her and pulled her close. It felt right, as if they'd never been apart. "You did good."

She shook her head against his shoulder. "I did horribly. He might have let me talk longer if I hadn't been so demanding when I first answered."

"No, I don't think it so. He let you talk to Max a long time."

"A long time?" She was surprised. "It wasn't even a minute."

"Abductors don't like to let the hostage have too much contact with the outside world. It makes them harder to subdue. Dawson said this guy was a professional, and I can see that he is." Travis turned his head so his lips were near her ear.

She could feel his warm breaths and the fast, hard beating of his heart.

"It's also better for the hostage not to have contact with anyone on the outside," he continued. "That way they won't waste so much of their energy screaming and crying and trying to figure out ways to escape. The sooner the hostage accepts his fate, the easier his life becomes."

Kate frowned. What was he talking about? Certainly not about Max. She pulled back and looked at him questioningly.

"What?" he said. He touched a damp spot on her cheek with a finger. It stung. She'd cried so much and wiped the tears away so often that the skin of her cheeks was raw.

She didn't say anything, she just kept watching him, noting, as she had the first time she'd taken a good look at him, the paleness, his drawn features, the dark circles under his eyes and the fact that his clothes hung from his shoulders, at least a size too large, if not more.

"Come on, Kate. You're looking at me with that *I'm a shrink, don't try anything* look." He held up a hand in a halfhearted gesture, as if trying to shield himself from her eyes.

"Oh, Travis. You weren't just on a mission,

were you?" she asked softly. "You were captured. You were held hostage."

He stared at her for a brief moment, his mouth set, his eyes flat.

She touched his shoulder, but he shrugged off her hand. "Talk to me," she said softly.

But he turned away. He walked over to the window and looked out on the darkness. "I had a tough mission, that was all. It was long and hard and lonely."

"Come on, Travis. I know it was more than that."

He turned back around and his face was expressionless. "You might be a shrink, but you're not my shrink. I left Walter Reed because I didn't want to hear all this. I'm sure not going to accept hearing it from you." The words were cutting, but Travis's tone was neutral, maybe even bordering on kind. Then, with no change in his expression or his tone, he asked, "How are you doing?"

Tears stung her eyes again. She massaged her temples with her fingertips. "I'm okay," she said, her voice thickening with the urge to cry. "I'm not sure if I'm going to ever stop crying, though." She gave a slight laugh. "Not until Max is home—" A little hiccup cut her sentence short and she felt what little resolve she had left crumble.

"You need to go to bed," Travis said, eyeing her closely. "You're exhausted. I know for a fact you were restless all last night. Between you and the wooden car sticking into my back, I didn't sleep very well, either. This stress is eating you up inside."

"I can't sleep," she said dismissively.

"Come on," he said with a smile. "Don't try to tell me that a physician doesn't have some kind of sleeping tablet or tranquilizer around the house." His voice went from neutral to gently amused.

She shook her head. "I don't want to take anything. What if something happens during the night?"

"Nothing's going to happen during the night. Besides, I'm here." His shoulders moved in a small shrug.

Kate started to protest again, but Travis spoke first. "I'll bet you haven't eaten all day, have you? Want some soup?"

She shook her head. She didn't think she could swallow anything.

"Okay. I know. I'll make you some hot chocolate while you go put on your pajamas and climb into bed."

"I should—" she began. "I need to—" But suddenly, her insides felt as though they'd run out of steam. Maybe she should have hot chocolate in bed and take something mild, just for tonight, just this one time, while Travis was here to take care of anything that might happen during the night. She felt guilty—for wanting to sleep while Max was being held by strangers, for allowing Travis to take over all her responsibilities.

He stepped close to her and lifted her chin with his finger. "You won't be any good to Max if you walk around in a fog," he said, as if he'd read her mind. "You need rest so you can work out what you're going to say in your evaluation of Stamps."

"You're right." She sighed. "I'll go to bed. I'm going to set my alarm for seven, so I can get into the office and work on the evaluation. I've got to schedule Stamps's interview, too. I haven't talked to him yet." Kate went into her bedroom and changed into a cami top and pajama bottoms, then went into the bathroom and opened the medicine cabinet. There was a bottle of children's cough medicine. She checked the label. Sure enough, it contained a mild antihistamine that was often used as a sleep aid. Reluctantly, she swallowed one child's dose and washed it down with a few sips of water from her bathroom glass. Then she got into bed and picked up the Nero Wolfe mystery she'd been reading, and stared at it as she waited for Travis to bring her a cup of hot chocolate.

She thought about Max and wondered if he'd had anything warm to drink before he went to bed. That set her eyes to burning and called up a nasty little headache at the base of her skull. She closed her eyes.

Some time later, she was aware of the lamp being turned off and Travis lying down on the bed next to her. In a sleepy haze, she turned and snuggled next to his warm body, resting her head on his shoulder.

"You awake?" he whispered, hardly more than mouthing the words.

"Kind of," she whispered back.

"Have you slept any?" he asked, pressing his face into her hair.

He felt her nod. "A little," she said. "I dreamed about Max."

"Good dreams?"

A tiny sob escaped from her throat. "Yes. Very good dreams." She snuggled closer to him. "Travis?"

"Yeah, hon?" The way she said his name, hesitantly, tentatively, he was sure she was going to ask him to get up. To sleep in the living room on the couch. That she wanted to be alone.

"Stay here."

That surprised him. "Here? You mean here, in bed?"

Her head moved up and down. "I need you close to me. I'm afraid if I'm alone I'll fall apart."

"Hey," he said, turning his head toward her, "I told you, I'm here for you. Anything you want, you just tell me and you got it."

She moved, pulling herself up and leaning over to kiss the side of his face. "Thank you," she said. "I don't know how you showed up at the exact moment I needed you."

He turned his head and pressed a kiss against her cheek. "I don't, either, but I'm—" His words were cut off by her lips, soft and tentative on his. He was afraid to move, afraid he'd break whatever spell had been cast between them. He closed his eyes and breathed in the strawberry scent of her hair and kissed her back, as softly and sweetly as she was kissing him. Despite the gentle sweetness, he began to become aroused. He suppressed a moan of frustration.

"Travis?" she whispered drowsily, her lips moving against his.

His pulse sped up. But he knew she was not only drowsy from the medication but exhausted. He set his jaw and forced himself to ignore the tantalizing feel of her soft, full mouth on his.

"I think I'm getting sleepy now...." Her words faded at the end and he felt the tension in her body relax as she fell asleep.

Now he did moan, low in his throat, then closed his eyes and listened to her soft, even breathing.

Chapter Seven

Kate woke up from a pleasant dream that she didn't remember. She opened her eyes and saw that it was light outside. She checked the clock on her bedside table. It was almost eight o'clock. How had she slept so late?

Then she remembered. Travis had talked her into taking a dose of Max's cough syrup last night. Plus the blue-gray color of the light seeping in at the edge of the blinds told her that it was cloudy, maybe even raining, outside.

Travis. She glanced at the pillow next to hers. There was an indentation there. A contented, safe feeling enveloped her as she remembered him turning off the light and lying down next to her. She remembered wanting to kiss him. Wanting to do more than kiss him. But she'd been so sleepy after her shower and the tiny dose of antihistamine. Closing her eyes, she let herself drift back to last night.

She had kissed him. She'd almost asked him to make love to her.

Then, with the swiftness of a blade cutting the air, her thoughts turned to Max and her safe, sexy, comfortable feelings dissolved. Her little boy wasn't safe or contented. He was in a cold, unfamiliar bed, and when he woke up, he'd want his mommy.

"Oh, Max," she whispered and pressed her palm against her chest. How much longer could she stand it without him? It had been two days. Before today, she'd have believed she couldn't survive for two hours without knowing where he was.

Now she faced the knowledge that it would be days until the trial started, and who knew how many days before the court ruled on whether Myron Stamps had been temporarily insane when he'd shot Paul Guillame. Her eyes filled with hot tears that scalded her tender skin as they slid down her cheeks.

She threw back the covers and got up. In the hall, she glanced into Max's room, half expecting to see Travis on the bed asleep, but he wasn't there. The couch in the living room was empty, as well.

"Travis?" She glanced back down the hall toward the bathroom, but its door was open and the light was out. "Travis?" she called again.

Her gaze snapped to the coffee table, where she'd left the phone last night, but it wasn't there.

Her hand pressed against her chest again as rising panic stole her breath. Where had he gone? To see his cousin again? The hand clutching her chest clenched into a fist and rose to her mouth. She pressed her knuckles against her teeth as a heavy emptiness settled deep in her heart.

For the first time in her life she understood what a patient meant when he or she said they were tempted to take a handful of tranquilizers and climb into bed. She was so tempted to sleep until all this was over and Max was home again. The realization that she could even consider putting her child's safety into someone else's hands while she withdrew from the world surprised and terrified her. She paced back and forth from the front door to the far wall of the living room and back again, wringing her hands as more tears coursed down her cheeks.

Her carefully constructed life was falling apart. She'd worked hard to make this house into a home for herself and Max. The two of them were a family. They'd been happy and contented and safe, until the kidnapper had snatched her little boy—her world—away from her. She paced, unaware of the time, her mind so scattered with fear and helplessness that she couldn't compose a rational thought.

Then, on one of her turns away from the front door, she heard it swing open. She whirled without thinking, her reaction an instinctive one, responding to the sound and nothing more.

Travis stepped inside. He was in sweatpants and a T-shirt and running shoes, and he was soaking wet. He stood on the tile floor just inside the door and wiped his face with a small towel, then rubbed it across his dripping, tousled hair.

"Travis," Kate whispered and flung herself into his arms.

"Hey—" Travis said, staggering backward. He caught himself and held his hands up and out. "I'm wet. Kate, what's the matter?" he asked, grasping her upper arms and setting her away enough so that he could look into her eyes.

"I woke up and didn't know where you were," she said.

"I couldn't sleep, so I went out for a run— well, actually it was a short walk, around the block. I was sure I'd be back before you woke up," he finished with a shrug.

Kate stared into his eyes and saw herself as he saw her. Immediately, she shook off the sleepy haze. What *was* the matter with her? She remembered the classic definition of insanity. Performing the same actions over and over and expecting different results.

How many times was she going to fall apart when he left? Granted, he hadn't been gone at all—this time. But she had enough anguish, enough heartache, just dealing with Max being abducted. There was no way she could survive getting sucked into missing Travis again.

"Sorry," she said coolly, not wanting to tell him the whole truth. "I woke up dreaming about Max." She shrugged. "I got upset." She did her best to hold Travis's gaze when his eyes narrowed. She knew that look. He knew she wasn't telling him the whole truth.

After a moment, he nodded. "I'm sorry I wasn't here."

She made a dismissive gesture. "I'm okay."

He looked down at his wet clothes. "I'm dripping all over the floor. I'm going to take a shower, if that's okay."

Kate nodded.

Travis stood there for another second or two, then headed for Max's bedroom, where he'd stowed his duffel bag.

"Travis?" she called.

"Yeah?" he said, stopping at the door.

"Where's the phone?"

"Oh." He fished in the pocket of his sweat-pants. "Here. I took it with me, in a plastic bag so it wouldn't get wet. I didn't want you to have to answer it alone."

She took the baggie with the phone inside it and stared at it as he headed into the hall bathroom, closing the door behind him.

Didn't want you to have to answer it alone. Kate grimaced as his words replayed in her head. "Don't be nice to me," she muttered.

She was still holding the phone, encased in its plastic bag, when it rang. She jumped, almost dropping it, and her heart leaped into her throat. It had to be the kidnapper. She glanced down the hall, but the bathroom door was still closed and she could hear the shower running. The phone rang for the third time. One more ring and it might go to voice mail. She couldn't take that chance. The kidnapper had warned her that she'd better be the one answering the phone the next time he called.

She flipped the phone open. The display said *Private Number.* She pressed the answer button. "Hello?" she said.

"This is Dawson Delancey. Is this Dr. Chalmet?"

Kate felt light-headed with relief. "Y-yes," she said breathlessly.

"I'm Travis's cousin. We've met a couple times in connection with cases."

"Yes, Mr. Delancey."

"Call me Dawson, please. May I speak to Travis?"

"He's—in the shower," she told him.

"Okay. I'd told him I'd call last night to find out what the kidnapper said, but I got tied up on a case."

"He was angry that you answered. He had told me not to tell anybody. He said that if someone else answered this time I would never see—" her breath hitched "—never see Max again."

"So did he let you talk to Max?"

"Yes, he did." To her dismay, her eyes filled with tears just thinking about his little voice saying, *Come get me, Mommy.*

"Did Max seem to be okay?" Dawson's voice turned gentle.

"I—I think so," Kate stammered. "He wanted his favorite car, but he said they gave him a stuffed bear and a train. And I heard a woman's voice in the background talking to him nicely. So I think he's being cared for. He didn't sound upset until—"

Just as she smelled the clean, fresh smell of soap and felt the brush of cotton terry cloth, Travis's hand covered hers. He pulled the phone away from her ear and pressed Speaker. "Dawson, it's Travis. You're on speaker with Kate and me."

"Hey, Trav. Kate was just telling me about how Max is doing. Kate, you were saying?"

"He was telling me about his toys when the man took the phone away from him," Kate said. "That was when he started getting upset—" Her voice broke. "He started crying and yelling for me. Then the man told the woman to *get the kid out of here.*"

"I see. I think that sounds promising."

"What did you find out?" Travis asked.

"Not much. But more than we had. I was right about the accent. Dusty has a program that compares speech patterns and pronunciation.

"The phone he used is a prepaid one and he bought it here, so I've sent the serial numbers to every phone store in the greater New Orleans area. Hopefully we'll get a hit."

"What about the car?"

"The numbers you got plus the distinctive graphics on the windshield hit. The sticker is a Chicago city sticker. Once we had that, we got the city clerk's office to run the partial plate for us. The car's registered to a Shirley Hixon. Lucas contacted his brother-in-law who's a prosecutor in Chicago. He'll get the woman checked out for us."

"You didn't tell him—" Kate started.

"Nope. Just told him I needed the info. We have a good arrangement," Dawson said. "He doesn't ask me any questions when I need a favor, and I don't ask him any when he needs a favor."

She sighed in relief.

"WHAT'S THAT noise in the background?" the man who'd hired Bentley Woods asked him. "Is somebody on TV strangling a cat?"

"Ha," Bent said with a grimace. "That kid's a spoiled little brat."

"Well, you better make sure he stays healthy. I thought you said your wife was taking care of him."

"My girlfriend."

"So anyway, like I was saying, one of the Delancey brats confronted Myron yesterday. I was out of the office or he'd have gotten to me, too. He asked Myron about Dr. Chalmet's kid, and mentioned the abduction."

"That must be the guy that answered the phone. Probably the same guy that's staying at her house."

"Staying? There's a Delancey staying at Dr. Chalmet's house?"

"Who?"

"Delancey. Didn't you hear what I just said? One of the Delanceys was nosing around, asking questions. And Stamps doesn't think he was just helping his little brother Harte with the case. He said the guy was acting like it was personal—*and* he mentioned the little boy."

"All I know is what you tell me," Bent said with exaggerated patience. "What's so special about these Delanceys?"

"You never heard of Con Delancey?"

"I have not. Who's Con Delancey?"

"Only one of the biggest, richest politicians ever in Louisiana. Most of his grandkids are cops. We don't need them snooping around in this."

"How come if everybody knows these Delanceys so well, nobody knows who went to Stamps's house?"

"I didn't see him. Myron did. He recognized him as a Delancey, but he didn't know which one."

"Oh. So he doesn't know and you don't know. What the hell's this got to do with me, anyhow? I'm doing the job you're paying me for. I'm taking care of the kid and making sure the doctor does what she's supposed to do."

"I'll compensate you for the additional work."

Bent started to ask what additional work, but

he knew what the man wanted him to do. And he liked the idea of more money. Besides, he'd already called a buddy of his in the Chicago P.D. to get them to run the Maryland license plate and see who the car was registered to. If he played his cards right, he could bill that to this guy, too. Maybe be could double his money. "Fine," he said grouchily. "Same fee."

"Same? You can't be serious—"

"Hey," Bent interrupted the man. "You're the one worried about the information getting out. All I gotta do is pack up and leave. You'll be stuck with the kid and trying to keep your nose clean at the same time."

"Okay, okay. But you'd better get back to me with some information and fast. Don't forget that a whole bunch of the Delanceys are police. Don't make 'em suspicious."

"I'll get your information. You get me my money."

"You'll get it when the job's done, along with the second half of the original fee. I'll call you back this afternoon."

"All right." Bent hung up. *Delanceys.* It sounded as if it would be in his best interest to find out who the Delanceys were and why they were interested in Dr. Kate Chalmet.

As he pocketed his phone, the kid's wailing went up a few hundred decibels. "Can't you shut that kid up?" he yelled. He was going to go crazy if he had to spend another minute in the same house as that spoiled brat. When he wasn't crying for his *mommy,* he was complaining about the toys Shirley had bought him or telling her he wanted milk not juice, or juice not milk.

"I'm taking the laptop and going out," he yelled over the kid's whining. "I'll be back later." *A lot later.*

"Bring me some more of that jambalaya you bought the other day."

"Aren't you sick of that stuff yet? I didn't like it the first time."

"You don't have to eat it," she countered. "Get it from the same restaurant. And get some more apple juice for Max."

Apple juice for Max, Bent mocked as he got in his car and headed to the small shopping center a couple miles from the trailer park. It had a grocery store, an office supply store, a coffee shop that sold pastries and sandwiches and a Chinese restaurant. He'd have to drive another three miles to get Shirley's jambalaya. But first he was going to have a latte and do a little business. He needed to check on that Maryland plate and he wanted to do some research on the Delanceys.

He'd left a message last night for a buddy of

his who was still with the Chicago P.D. By the time he reached the coffee shop, got his coffee and signed on to the internet, his phone rang. It was his buddy calling him back. "Hey, pal, what's shaking?" Bent asked when he answered.

"Not much. What's up with you?"

"Nothing new. Still scraping by with a couple private jobs. You know how it is."

"Yeah. So I ran that plate you gave me. The car's registered to a Travis Delancey. I dug a little deeper and found out he's active military."

"No kidding? So he's stationed in D.C.? Is that why his car has a Maryland license plate?"

"Got no idea. You know all I know now."

"Okay. That helps," Bent said. "Thanks, pal, I owe you one."

"Yeah, you do."

Bent sipped his coffee and typed the name Travis Delancey into a search engine. He found out he was the third son of Robert Delancey, older son of the late Senator Robert Connor "Con" Delancey. There were lots of news stories, comments and blogs about his grandfather, Con Delancey, who apparently was murdered by his personal assistant twenty-something years before.

Bent was surprised at how much information was online about the family, especially the grandfather. Con Delancey had shaken hands with a lot of famous and infamous people— politicians, foreign dignitaries, celebrities. His grandchildren were all over the internet, too. Bent paged through hundreds of family photos, school pictures, candid paparazzi-like shots until he was practically cross-eyed. It didn't take long for him to see that they were a state-sized version of the Kennedy family. Both lines were revered as American *royalty* and yet their histories were fraught with scandal. As with the Kennedys, the Delanceys were a handsome bunch, with a definite familial resemblance. Bent saw how Stamps could have recognized a member of the family even if he'd never met that particular Delancey before.

But as much information as was out there, the girl, Cara Lynn, was the only obvious connection between the Delanceys and Dr. Kate Chalmet. When he entered *Chalmet and Delancey* into the search engine, he found the same information he'd discovered before. The doctor and Cara Lynn Delancey had entered LSU the same year.

College. That was a thought. Maybe there was more than one Delancey family member who went to LSU. He entered *Travis Delancey graduated LSU.* The search engine asked him if he'd meant *Delancy.* He amended his search to *Travis Delancey college LSU*. That brought up a list of Delancey grandchildren and where they'd gone to college. Travis Delancey, about halfway down the list, had LSU beside his name. *Bingo*.

Bent then searched images for *Chalmet and Delancey and LSU*. There were several of Cara Lynn and Kate, together at various school functions. But nothing else.

He looked closely at the photos of Cara Lynn Delancey. It wasn't that much of a stretch from Dr. Chalmet being friends with Cara Lynn Delancey to the theory that Dr. Chalmet's little boy was Travis Delancey's son, especially considering he'd shown up in New Orleans within hours of the kid's kidnapping.

Excitement churned in Bent's gut, along with the espresso drink. He saved the link to the photo in his bookmarks and shut down the laptop. Then he walked over to the office supply store and got an enlargement of the photo of the doctor with Cara Lynn Delancey.

Back in his car, he studied the picture. He could easily make a case that the whiny brat was related to the Delancey girl. There was a striking resemblance. Yep, the kid could definitely be a Delancey. Bent felt his scalp burn with excitement. This little tidbit could turn out to be a gold mine.

AFTER KATE LEFT for her office, Travis headed to Baton Rouge to confront Congressman Gavin Whitley at his office. When he walked into the suite, he saw that the door to the plush inner office was open.

He didn't stop at the secretary's desk. Instead he walked right around it.

The fiftysomething woman said, "May I help—?"

But by then he'd left her in his dust and was in the congressman's office. Whitley sat behind his desk, staring out the window.

Travis quickly took in the items on the top of the dark wood desk. They included several legal-sized manila file folders haphazardly scattered across the surface, a Styrofoam take-out container and a cell phone. "Congressman Whitley," he said.

Whitley's head snapped around. "What?" He blinked as his eyes focused. "Who are you?"

"I think you know," Travis said, "but I'll introduce myself. I'm Travis Delancey. I spoke to your colleague, Myron Stamps, yesterday."

The man's Adam's apple bobbed as he swallowed. He leaned forward and started to lift the receiver on his desk phone, but then his gaze snapped to the office door behind Travis.

Travis figured it was the secretary at the

door, but he knew better than to turn around and look.

"Congressman, I'm sorry. I couldn't—"

"It's all right, Mary. Call security please, to escort this—gentleman—out of the building."

"Yes, sir."

"Tell the guards no hurry, Mary. I'll just need a few minutes," Travis said.

Mary looked at each of them in turn, then compressed her already thin lips as she left the office and closed the heavy wooden door behind her.

Travis calculated that he had two minutes at most, if he wanted to get away without being detained and asked a lot of questions. "I have one simple request," he said to the congressman. "Return Dr. Chalmet's child to her immediately and she won't press criminal charges. I haven't decided what I will or won't do yet."

Whitley's brows drew down and he shook his head. "I have no idea what you're talking about."

"I don't have the time or the patience to play this game, *Congressman*. I don't have a security force to call, but I do know several police detectives. I can call them. They'll be glad to come over here and put you in handcuffs for kidnapping a child—a federal offense, by the way. Or maybe you're ready to start talking, right now."

Whitley's lips began to tremble, but he stuck to his guns. "I will repeat. I have no idea what you're talking about."

Travis reached out and picked up the cell phone. "Really? I must be mistaken, then," he drawled as he looked at the recent call log on the phone. There were several calls that appeared routine—other congressmen and senators, his wife, his country club. But there was one that was labeled *Unknown.* Travis's pulse skittered. "So this recent seven-minute phone call right here?" He held up the phone's screen so Whitley could see. "The one that says B.W. Who's that?"

"I'm afraid I don't remember that call," Whitley said. "Perhaps it was a wrong number."

"Wrong number? You programmed it into your phone, and this call is seven minutes long."

"Aah, yes. I believe that's—a real estate agent. That's right. I'm thinking of buying a cabin on the lake."

Travis laughed. "I don't think so." He pulled out his phone and called Dawson. "Hang on just a minute," he said to Whitley.

When Dawson answered, Travis said, "Hey. I'm with Whitley. Just took a look at his phone and found out he's been talking to our friend. Want the number?"

"Absolutely."

Travis read the phone number off to Dawson. "It's labeled B.W."

Whitley started to rise. "You can't do that—"

Travis glared at him. He sat.

Dawson said, "Great. This'll simplify a lot of things."

"Thanks." Travis hung up, then deleted the listing from Whitley's phone. He turned the congressman's phone over, took out the battery and dropped it on the floor. "Oh, no!" Travis exclaimed and took a step, stomping on the battery and smashing it. "Look what I've done. I'm so sorry. You'll have to get a new one." He set the phone back on the desk and dug a couple bills out of his pocket. "Here's some money for your new battery. Again, I'm truly sorry." He glanced at his watch and saw that it had been just over two minutes since he'd walked past the secretary.

Travis headed for the door. "When I find the kidnapper, he's going to be begging the police to let him tell all about who hired him and why. Oh, by the way, I hope you had that number memorized. Because it's not in your phone anymore."

To his satisfaction, Whitley's mouth dropped open as he realized Travis had deleted the phone number. He slipped through the office door and closed it behind him.

Travis scooted past Mary's desk, giving her a half salute. "Thanks, Mary. Tell the security guys I hate it that I missed them."

Mary was apparently struck speechless, because she didn't say a word as Travis left the office and headed toward the rear of the building. He was counting on the guards to come in the front. He slipped down the rear fire stairs and circled the building just in time to see two uniformed men heading up the steps at the front of the building. He waited until they'd entered, then jogged to his car and took off, wondering if Whitley was planning to tell them that a Delancey had come into his office, destroyed his phone battery and walked out.

Once he was back in traffic and headed toward Kate's, he called Dawson again. "Is it too early to ask if you got anything from that number?"

"Five-and-a-half minutes? Nah. Not too early," Dawson said wryly. "Dusty's already done some computer magic and traced the number to a very busy store on Canal Street. Nobody at the shop recalls who bought it, but the store has been helping the NOPD trace the cell phones of a drug ring, so they've been trying to get license plates when they can."

"They have the kidnapper's plate?"

"Yep. We caught a break there. The plate was partially obscured by mud but it's a Cook County, Illinois, plate and the first two numbers match the numbers you saw. When we checked with the Cook County DMV, they confirmed the make and model."

"So it's the same vehicle I saw. It belongs to the kidnapper."

"Yep. We've been trying to pick up the phone's GPS signal but we haven't had any luck. He must turn it off when he's not using it. But we will. When we call him, Dusty will pinpoint him to the nearest tower, or triangulate off three if we're lucky."

"Great," Travis said.

"Do you have time to drive over here to Biloxi this evening? We could talk about when to get Lucas or Ryker involved."

"Not tonight. I'm going to be late getting back to Kate's house and I don't like her to be there alone in the dark. And I'm not so sure about getting them involved."

"Okay, but if you try to do something dangerous by yourself, I'll sic every Delancey on the police force on you if you try."

"Yeah," Travis said with a wry chuckle. "I hear you."

Chapter Eight

Kate had spent the morning reading the rest of the police reports and witness statements in the shoot-out at Paul Guillame's house. In the afternoon, she'd interviewed both Stamps and Guillame. The interviews had been an exercise in futility. It was as though the two of them had made some kind of pact to say as little as possible about the shooting.

Stamps spent most of his interview swearing he didn't remember anything after the shooting started. He acknowledged that the police had found gunshot residue on his hands and clothes and that a bullet from his gun had been removed from Paul Guillame's left upper thigh. But according to Stamps, he didn't even remember having the gun, although he did keep it in his glove compartment, since he never knew when he might be driving through rough neighborhoods. *I like to visit the neighborhoods of all my constituents,* he had told her.

I feel it's important for the people I represent to see me.

She'd thanked him for coming in, and when he was gone, she'd just stared at the bound notebook where she normally jotted her impressions when doing these types of interviews. She had no idea what to write down. It would be a bald-faced lie to say that Stamps appeared insane. Whether he had temporarily *blacked out* as he'd said he did once the shooting started, she couldn't say for sure, but she knew she'd have a hard time maintaining her credibility with the District Attorney's office if she found that he had definitely been temporarily insane when he'd shot Paul Guillame.

Then, Paul Guillame's interview hadn't gone any better. Guillame declared that Stamps had appeared glassy-eyed and confused when he'd taken the shot. "I could swear he wasn't even looking at me," Guillame had told her. He denied any recollection of Stamps yelling a discriminatory epithet at him at any time.

"You'd swear under oath that he wasn't looking at you?" she'd asked.

"Well, maybe not under oath," he'd prevaricated, "but he sure looked dazed and confused."

Now, as Kate drove into her driveway, she was disappointed to see that Travis's car was not there. She went inside and locked the door behind her, then set down the two grocery sacks she'd brought in with her. She'd decided to make Travis's favorite, spaghetti, and a salad. He needed to put some meat back on his bones.

As she put the sauce on to cook and added basil, bay leaves, oregano, lots of garlic and olive oil, her eyes filled with tears. She and Travis had dreamed up this recipe in her dorm room in college, and cooked it in the microwave. She'd made it for Max and herself many times. Now as the sauce heated, the tangy smell nearly broke her heart.

Picking up the spoon, she stirred the sauce again and turned it down to low. Surely Travis wouldn't be much longer getting home. She had already stored the Parmesan cheese and a half gallon of milk in the refrigerator, then pulled the remaining item—a package of Oreo cookies—out of the grocery bag. She was determined to make Travis eat as much as he could hold.

Her cell phone rang. She grabbed it out of her purse and answered it without looking, thinking it was Travis, letting her know when he'd be there.

"Dr. Chalmet." It was that voice. Kate's pulse hammered.

"Yes," she said breathlessly as her mind

raced. Why wasn't Travis here? How much longer would he be? He'd promised to be back before dark but this time of the year, it didn't get completely dark until after eight o'clock.

She held the phone pressed tightly against her ear, listening for Max's voice in the background, but she didn't hear him. "I want to talk to my son," she said.

"Oh, Doc, are you going to start with that again?" the kidnapper said. "I thought I told you, *I* will decide when you can talk to your little boy. Not you. If you'd just *shut up* and listen, you might get more of what you want than if you persist in *hounding me* about talking to the kid. Do you understand?"

"Yes," she said through gritted teeth.

"Good. Now listen to me."

She waited.

"Are you listening?" he snapped.

"Yes," she said, suppressing the urge to say *yes, sir* sarcastically.

"Good. I'm a real good researcher, Doc. Real good. Do you want to know what I found out today?"

Kate's teeth were still gritted, so tightly her temple was beginning to pound. "Yes, please," she said.

The kidnapper laughed. It wasn't a pleasant sound. "Okay then, since you're being so polite." He paused and took a deep breath. "I know who the kid's daddy is."

"What?" she said, startled. "What do you mean?" It was a stupid response, but right now her thoughts were spinning around in her head so fast it was making her dizzy. She couldn't keep up with most of them, they were spinning so fast. But every once in a while an actual phrase or question materialized.

How had he found out? Nobody knew, right? Who did he think was Max's dad? Why did it matter? What would she say if he were right?

"Travis," she mouthed silently. *Where are you?*

"What do you think I mean, Doc? I mean I *know* who the kid's *father* is. Don't you want me to tell you?"

Kate's stomach churned with apprehension. He was leading up to something—but what?

Travis, help. I need you.

"Okay," the kidnapper said. "I'll take your silence as a yes. Your son is—a Delancey." He announced it with the intonation of a game show host saying *And the answer is—*

Kate dropped onto one of the counter stools as though a thousand-pound weight had been dropped on her chest. She couldn't breathe. Every effort to pull air into her lungs made her chest ache and tighten even more. "I don't understand." It was all she could think of to say. And saying it used up every last tiny breath of air in her lungs. She held the phone away from her mouth and took a deep, openmouthed inhale.

"Doc? You okay?" the man asked, with what sounded like a grin in his voice. "Did I surprise you?"

For a moment Kate couldn't speak. She didn't think she had enough air. She just sat there, her palm splayed across her chest, and tried to take long, slow breaths. As a psychiatrist, she knew what was happening to her. She was on the verge of hyperventilating. If she didn't get it under control, she'd be gasping and heaving for air. She didn't want to have to breathe into a paper bag or into her cupped hands. She wanted to be able to talk to this awful man—find out why he was telling her this and what he was going to do.

"N-no," she stammered—not a complete lie. She'd been afraid he'd really known. It was useless to question how he'd found out. Useless to worry about what he planned to do with the information.

"That's what I thought. Well, I must congratulate you on having managed to have a Delancey kid. I didn't know much about the Delanceys before, but now I do. Very impressive. I wonder how much the kid's grandparents would be willing to cough up to save their first grandbaby. Yep, I know that, too. Little Max is the first great-grandchild of Con Delancey, right?" He laughed. "Or maybe I should say the first one anybody *knows* about."

Kate didn't hear anything after *cough up to save their first grandbaby.* Her hand moved from her chest to cover her open mouth, just in time to stop the scream that was crawling its way up her throat. *Oh, no, please. No, no, no.*

"Apparently you're speechless, eh, Doc? That's okay. You need time to process what I've told you. Time to calm down. No sense in making you talk to the kid right now. It would just upset both of you."

"No-o-o," she sobbed. "Please, let me ta-talk to him."

"Nah," the kidnapper said. "I can't stand to listen to the little brat cry."

"Please," she whispered.

"But I tell you what. You let your baby-daddy know what I know, and we'll all have a great little conversation soon, 'kay?"

"Wait!" she cried. "Wait, please."

She heard a sigh. "What? I'm not letting you talk to your kid."

"Please, don't call the Delanceys. Give me

some time. I can get money. I can pay you. Just please don't call them."

"And what's going to convince me that you have the kind of money the Delanceys have?" he asked.

"I don't. But—" How could she convince him? Maybe the same thing that made her not want the Delanceys involved would make sense to him. "You don't want to get mixed up with the Delanceys," she said firmly. "Why do you think I've tried to keep my son's father a secret all this time, when I could go to them and probably not have to work another day in my life?"

"I don't know. You love your job?" The kidnapper was obviously getting impatient with her.

"Because their influence spreads all over this state. You don't want them onto you, I can promise you that. There are at least four policemen in the immediate family, plus a prosecutor, plus a very dangerous private investigator. Not to mention an army Special Forces operative. How many of those do you want on your trail?"

There was a pause. "How do I know they're not already?"

"You don't. You're just going to have to trust me, like I'm offering to trust you."

"All right. What's your proposal, and more important, how much money can you get me?"

Kate tried to think fast. She knew how much money she had, down to the penny, and it wasn't going to be enough to tempt this man. A small inheritance from her parents plus the money she'd been saving for Max's college fund would add up to $73,000. Not even a drop in the bucket, when measured next to the funds of the Delanceys.

"A quarter of a million," she said as confidently as she could.

"Really," he said, disbelievingly. "On your own, without the Delanceys, you've got two-hundred-and-fifty big ones?"

"I'll need a day—maybe more, depending on the bank—but yes." She heard a slight flutter in her voice. Dear God, she hoped the kidnapper hadn't heard it.

"I don't like it. How do I know you're not just stalling me to give your boyfriend time to get his detective brother on my trail?"

"You don't. Like I told you, you're going to have to trust me."

"Yeah? Why? How're you going to convince me to trust you?"

Kate took a halting, shaky breath. "Because you have the one thing in the world that I would give my life for," she said. "You have my son."

The phone clicked and went dead.

"No!" she cried, jerking the phone from her

ear and looking at the display. "No, please!" But the call had been disconnected. After a couple tries, she pulled up the phone log and saw the same notation she'd seen every time she talked to the kidnapper. *Private Number.* She pressed Star-Six-Nine—nothing. She pressed Call—nothing. She clicked Edit, Store, every button she could find to press, except Delete, but nothing worked.

She slammed the phone down on the counter, then sat with her head in her hands.

What was she going to do now that the kidnapper knew that Max was a Delancey? If she thought her child was in danger before, it was nothing compared to now. Her heart felt as though the kidnapper had reached into her chest and ripped it out of her when he'd hung up.

She had no idea what he was going to do. Had he rejected her offer? Was he convinced he couldn't trust her? But if he thought the Delanceys were already onto him, wouldn't her plan still be better than him trying to get money out of them?

She turned her gaze up to the ceiling, wishing she could force an answer from heaven.

At that instant, she heard a key in the front door. It opened and Travis walked in.

"Wow!" he said, grinning. "It smells great in here. Spaghetti, right?"

WHEN HE LOOKED into Kate's eyes, he stopped short. "Is everything okay?"

She pointed at the phone. "You wa-want to know who that was?" she said bitterly, not even trying to stop the tears that welled in her eyes and slid down her cheeks.

"Who?" Travis approached her gingerly.

"The kidnapper."

Travis nodded. "I didn't mean for you to have to talk to him by yourself. I'm sorry I didn't make it home earlier. What did he say? Did you get to talk to Max?" He held out his arms.

She shook her head quickly, back and forth and back and forth. "No," she said. "No. You stay away from me."

"What happened? I don't understand."

"Really?" she said, still shaking her head. "You're going to stand there and tell me you have no idea what you've done? My baby is in danger and it's because of *you*." She clenched her fists and worked very hard at channeling all her fear and despair and aching emptiness into anger at Travis. But it still hurt just as bad.

"Kate, tell me what he said."

"You had to go and get involved, didn't y-you?" she cried. "Had to get right in the m-middle of it and g-get your *cousin* involved."

Travis regarded her with frank bewilderment and spread his hands. "I'm not sure what's happening here. Why don't we sit down on the couch and you can tell—"

"Don't!" she cried. "Don't patronize me. It's you and your damn rich family. It's always been my biggest fear. Why do you think I never went to your parents about Max? I never even told Cara Lynn, and she's my best friend. And now—everything I feared has come true." She blotted her face with the sleeve of her blouse. "He *knows!*"

Travis just stared at her.

"He—knows!" she screamed, pointing to the phone.

Then as calmly as she could, she said, "The kidnapper knows that Max is your child. He's going to call your parents and see how much they'd pay to make sure their *first* great-grand-child is safe."

Travis's face twisted into a mask of horror as her words sank in. "Oh my God," he muttered. "How did he find out?"

"You tell me," she grated. "Maybe he saw you with Dawson."

Travis shook his head. "No. He didn't see us. Even if I didn't notice him, Dawson would have."

"Well, he found out somehow."

Travis's forehead creased in a frown. "Stamps or Whitley must have talked."

"Stamps or Whitley? What are you talking about?" she asked. *Stamps?* She didn't like the expression on Travis's face any more than what he'd said. He looked chagrined and he wouldn't meet her gaze. She saw his throat move as he swallowed.

"I—went to see Stamps yesterday, after I talked to Dawson. I figured he needed to know that we were onto him—"

"You went to *see* him?" The anger she'd been searching for earlier, that she'd hoped would sweep away the empty ache of missing her child, now began to burn through her. It didn't get rid of the emptiness, but it felt good. "You went to see Senator Stamps. Do you have any idea what you've done?"

"Now, Kate—" Travis began.

"Stop talking!" she snapped, slicing a hand through the air. "Don't even pretend you have an explanation for this." She stepped over to the stove and turned off the spaghetti sauce, congratulating herself for having presence of mind enough to do that. She closed her eyes.

As much as she wished she could depend on Travis, she knew from experience she couldn't. She was the one who always handled things. So she would handle this, too. But she was going to need all the information she could get. With a huge sigh, she asked, "Who's Whitley?"

"Congressman Gavin Whitley. He's actually the one who hired the kidnapper. Dawson traced down the kidnapper's phone number and found out where he bought it. I found that same number on Whitley's phone. So now, with that information and using your phone, Dawson should be able to zero in on where they're keeping Max."

"Please, Travis. I don't want you to do anything else. I don't want Dawson to do anything else. I'm taking care of it, just like I always have. When you walked out on me in college. When I found myself pregnant with your child. If there's one thing I know how to do, it's how to get along without you."

"Come on, Kate. You don't have to—"

"I swear to you on your child's life, if you don't leave this alone right now, I will take Max and move away from here and you will never, ever find us. You will *never* see your child." Kate felt sick, saying those words. It wasn't what she wanted. It had never been her choice to raise her child alone. She'd always thought that one day he would come back and they would be a family.

But she knew now that her vision of them as a family was a pipe dream. The reality was what it had always been. Travis would walk away and Kate would handle it.

She lifted her chin and glared at him. "I don't have much that's mine. But Max is my son and this is my house. I want you to leave, now."

Travis stared at Kate, trying to process everything she'd said. He knew how many times he'd let her down. But he wasn't going to let her down this time. He wished there was a way to tell her that, to make her stop and look at him and see—not the boy he'd been, too angry and too immature to be responsible. But the man he'd become. Who knew how to channel his anger. Who knew what was worth living for—and even dying for. He'd sat in that filthy dark room where his enemy had kept him for five months, completely alone. He'd faced his shortcomings, his demons, his fears. And now, at last, he knew that only love could heal what was wrong with him. He hoped he wasn't too late in recognizing it.

"Kate, don't do this. We can get him back. I promise you."

But her chin just went up another fraction of an inch and her glare never wavered.

He shook his head, held out a hand in supplication, then when she ignored it, let it drop to his side. Then he walked past her into their child's room and threw his clothes into his duffel bag before hoisting it over his shoulder. When he came back into the living room, she was still standing in the same place, but her head was now bowed and her eyes were closed.

He walked past her to the front door, then turned around. "Kate, you're telling me to leave, but I swear to you, *I* am *not* walking out on you." She didn't react. "Damn it, Kate. Look at me."

Slowly she raised her head and met his gaze. Her face was awash with both a profound sadness and a steely determination.

"I am not walking out. I've got this phone, and you've got the number in yours. Call me and I promise I will be here before you hang up the phone. That is my solemn promise to you—on our son's life."

Travis didn't miss the irony of declaring to Kate that he was not walking out on her in one breath and in the next, turning around and leaving. But he'd told her the truth. Even if she never wanted to lay eyes on him again, he was not going to leave her to face the kidnapper alone. He would be right here, watching her, making sure she was safe.

She had hit him where it hurt, with those comments about him walking out. He hadn't realized until she'd said it, but that was exactly what he'd done—twice. He certainly had not forgotten the first time. She'd brought up marriage and he'd reacted with such immediate anger, he'd scared not only her, but himself. So he'd done what his older brother Lucas had hounded him about for years. How many times had Lucas said it? *You ought to join the military, Trav. They'd whip that anger right out of you.*

The army and later Special Forces had given him confidence, skills and a deep understanding of his physical, mental and emotional self. Above all, they'd taught him to channel his anger into a different, more helpful energy and to use that energy to maintain an ironclad control in order to beat every enemy. Lucas had been right.

Now he had to draw on every bit of that control to save his son and keep Kate safe, whether she wanted him to or not. He didn't know what she was planning to do, but he did know that he wasn't about to let her deal with the kidnapper alone.

Sitting in his car in front of her house, he dialed Dawson's number. When Dawson answered, he said, "Have you got a vehicle I can borrow?"

"I've got several. What do you need it for?" As usual, Dawson was prepared for almost anything.

"I need something that won't stand out in Kate's neighborhood. I'm going to be watching her house. I'm afraid she's made some kind of arrangement with the kidnapper."

There was an almost undetectable pause on the other end of the call. Then Dawson said, "Sure. In the parking lot next to the warehouse where we met, there's a late-model white van. There are various magnetic signs inside, along with a couple pairs of coveralls and a few other items. Use the large magnetic sign that says City of New Orleans. If you wear the white coverall, maybe a Saints baseball cap and sunglasses and carry a clipboard, you can hang around all day. If somebody asks you what you're doing, tell them you're assessing the need for house numbers on the curb in front of the houses."

"Not bad," Travis said. "It'll take me a while to pick up those things."

"No need. They're in the van. The coverall fits me so it'll be okay on you."

"Great. Where are the keys?"

"Upstairs, in the cabinet over the microwave."

"Thanks, Dawson."

"No problem. Listen, we're almost ready to make the call to the kidnapper. Dusty has altered the data that will be sent to the kidnapper's phone so that he'll think the call is from Whitley. But we'll only have one chance, and it'll be a slim one, because as soon as he realizes it's not Whitley, he'll hang up and won't answer again. So we have to plan when we want to make the call. Dusty is tracking the GPS coordinates of the phone. As soon as he answers, she'll triangulate the signal."

"What do you think?" Travis asked. "Should we get the police involved?"

"Not officially. I'll talk to Ryker and fill him in. See if he'll work with us unofficially. Lucas already knows about the situation. He just doesn't know you're involved. With the two of them, we'll have the city and the North Shore covered."

"What about the locals?"

"So far we don't know which local police

department we'll be dealing with. We'll bring them in, but obviously it'll be at the last second."

"They're not going to be happy," Travis said.

Dawson nodded grimly. "No kidding. And once they know about the kidnapping—"

"It becomes their case and we have no more control."

"Exactly."

Travis sighed. "Kate's going to hate me even more before this is all over."

"That'll be better than her being destroyed by grief, if she can't save her child."

TRAVIS WAS AT Kate's house by eight o'clock the next morning. He was in Dawson's van, dressed in the white coverall and ready to look busy and preoccupied as he studied his clipboard. When he turned onto her street, he saw the dark green sedan that belonged to the kidnapper.

His hands tightened on the steering wheel. There was nothing he wanted more than to go drag the man out of his car by his collar, toss him onto the ground and stand on his neck until he revealed Max's location. But Travis knew expert interrogation techniques from both sides—as a Special Forces operative and as a hostage. He knew that there was a very real chance that the man wouldn't give up the information no matter what. There was also the risk of alerting his partner by preventing a phone call or some other prearranged signal.

No. Travis had to work slowly and methodically to be sure the kidnapper wasn't alerted. The last thing they needed was for Max to be harmed or whisked away to another location. So he casually drove past the kidnapper's car and stopped a dozen houses away near the end of the block. Travis wasn't skilled at tailing, so he was going to have to be extremely careful as he followed Kate and the kidnapper.

It was eight-thirty before Kate came out of the house and locked the door. She didn't pay any attention to the car with the real estate sign on its side, parked a few houses away from hers. She backed out of her driveway and drove off. The kidnapper pulled away from the curb and followed her.

Travis followed the green sedan at a safe distance. He expected Kate to drive to her office, but she didn't. Instead, she led them to a bank and parked in its parking lot. Again, the green sedan parked half a block away and Travis drove on past and turned at the next light. He pulled into a small parking lot and quickly changed the magnetic sign from *City of New Orleans* to *Upton Upholstery—Uptown Style for 15 Years.* He slipped out of the coverall, took off the Saints cap but left his sunglasses on, then made the block and parked at a fast-food restaurant across the street from the bank. He walked into the restaurant and bought a burger and a soft drink and went back to the van to eat while he waited.

He knew what Kate was doing and he wasn't happy about it. He'd done what he could to keep her from having to deal directly with the kidnapper, at the very least trying to be there when he called.

He couldn't believe she had enough money to come close to tempting the kidnapper away from Travis's wealthy family. Even on a psychiatrist's earnings, there was little chance she could scrape up a decent fraction of what the kidnapper might demand from the Delanceys. What frightened him the most, though, was that the kidnapper would decide that two birds were better than one and he'd kidnap Kate, as well.

And he knew that for all his training and all his carefully honed restraint, he would kill the man if he hurt Kate or their son.

Kate was inside the bank for over two hours. Travis had moved from the fast-food parking lot to a side street a couple blocks away from the kidnapper where he couldn't see the bank's parking lot. When the kidnapper pulled away from the curb, Travis followed him. As soon as they came to a straightaway, he saw Kate's car in front of the green sedan. She went directly from the bank to a credit union, where she only spent about forty-five minutes. Then she went directly to her office, oblivious to the two vehicles following her.

Once she walked inside her office building, the kidnapper, who'd been idling at the curb half a block away, pulled into the street and headed away. Travis started the van and followed him. He wasn't sure if following the kidnapper was the best idea, especially in a decade-old minivan, but he couldn't pass up the chance that the kidnapper might lead him to where he was keeping Max.

The kidnapper got on Interstate 10 and took the Airline Highway exit. He was heading to his hideout. Travis was sure of it. Now he had a decision to make. He was going to follow the man and he would find out where he was keeping Max. But what was he going to do then?

He knew how to move through deep forest or open desert nearly undetectably. With the proper equipment, he could pick locks and cut window glass without making a sound. But he held little hope that those skills would help him. Even if he could sneak into the place where they were holding Max, even if he could neutralize the kidnapper and his partner, how would he approach his son? To Max, he would be nothing more than another stranger.

Suddenly, the green sedan sped up, darting from one lane to another, avoiding cars. Travis's pulse sped up. The kidnapper had spotted him. He gunned the van's engine, but there was a dismaying lack of pickup. Still, he floored it. He wasn't going to lose the kidnapper if he could help it. He watched the speedometer creep higher, too slowly, and listened to the van's engine struggle. Ahead of him, the sedan was putting more and more distance between them. Airline Highway was a long, straight road, but as the sedan grew smaller and smaller, it became harder for Travis to keep his eye on it.

The van's engine was straining. The speedometer appeared to be stalled at ninety. Travis focused on the road ahead, but now he couldn't spot the dark green sedan at all. He didn't give up, though. If he couldn't see the sedan, he was certain the sedan couldn't see him. So he kept driving, past Kenner, past the airport and farther, into LaPlace, then on until he saw the signs for the Maurepas Swamp. He slowed the van down and took the next exit.

Stopping on the side of the road, he slammed

the steering wheel with the heel of his hand. "Damn it!" he shouted, then pressed his palms against his eyes. He knew there was no way the van could have ever caught the sedan, but still he felt as though he'd failed his son. As though he'd failed Kate. All he could do now was head back. As he drove, he mentally cataloged each exit, and pinpointed the spot where he'd lost sight of the kidnapper's car. He had driven almost thirty miles by the time he reached the swamp, where he decided it was useless to go farther. He doubted the hideout was in there, so it had to be one of the exits after the point where Travis had lost him.

He drove to the warehouse and parked the van, then went upstairs to use Dawson's computer. Using Google Maps, he marked the exits that the kidnapper might have used, then forwarded a copy to Dawson and printed a copy for himself.

Within a couple minutes, Dawson called him. "So what am I looking at here?" he asked.

"I followed the kidnapper this afternoon. He went out Airline Highway. Of course I lost him around the Highway 51 exit, since his car was a whole lot faster than the van."

"Did he get off at 51?"

"No. He was still going. That was the point at which I lost sight of him. I drove on until I entered the Maurepas Swamp, but after a few minutes of driving and not seeing a single side road, I figured if he was hiding in there, I'd never find him. I guess I could have gotten off at every exit and searched for his car, but that'd be like a needle in a haystack, so I thought it might be better to get this information to you."

"I'm glad you did. Dusty's almost ready to make the call. But we've got to get everything coordinated. We can't afford to waste our only chance," Dawson said. "We'll coordinate from the warehouse."

"Okay," Travis said. "When?" He was ready, but he needed Kate to be involved. She was furious with him for going behind her back, but if she knew they were ready to close in on the kidnapper, she'd want to be there. She'd really hate him if they went in and she wasn't there for Max.

"Preferably tonight. Then we can make our move at daylight tomorrow, hopefully while they're still asleep."

"You're sure you can pinpoint the location that closely?"

"I hope so. I think your map is going to help, plus I've got my best agent, MacEllis Griffin, standing by in a helicopter."

"A helicopter?"

"He's going to do a flyover of the triangulated area and try to spot the sedan."

Travis was impressed, although he should have known Dawson would think of everything.

"I need to let Kate know what we're doing. I know she'll want to be there for Max."

Dawson paused for a split second. "Now, Travis, Ryker and Reilly are going to be handling the ambush and taking the kidnappers into custody. This is off the books, but Ryker is arranging to have a female officer there to take charge of Max."

"That's not going to work for Kate," Travis said with a wry laugh.

"Well, how you handle Kate is up to you. And trust me, I understand completely about a woman who won't sit by and let you do the rescuing. But we don't know anything about this guy. I doubt Ryker is going to want either you or Kate on the scene."

Travis thought maybe his cousin could convince Kate that she should wait until the danger was over, but he'd be damned if they kept *him* from being there. He might not be a cop, but he was probably better armed barehanded than they were with their weapons.

"Oh, and I heard from Lucas," Dawson went on. "He got some information from his friend in Chicago. It seems that a woman named Shirley Hixon shares an address with an ex-cop named Bentley Woods. He was fired several years ago for taking bribes and protection money. Since then he's been a suspect in a couple murders that seemed to be *gun for hire,* but in both cases the ID was weak, so they couldn't prosecute. He said that Woods claims to be doing private-investigator work, but that word on the street is he'll do just about anything if the price is right."

"He sounds dangerous. I don't like it."

"We think the Hixon woman is taking care of your boy. She and Woods have shared the same address for nine years. If they've been doing kidnappings for hire for that long, I'm amazed they've never been caught."

"Yeah, well, that's going to change this time."

He heard Dawson sigh through the phone. "Just don't forget what I said. Ryker's not going to want you there for the takedown."

"Ryker and I will have to have a conversation about that," Travis said.

Chapter Nine

By the time Kate got home that evening, it was after six o'clock. She'd spent all morning at the bank. She'd gone straight to the bank manager and asked him for a loan of two hundred thousand dollars. She offered the house she'd inherited from her folks as collateral and when that didn't work, she tried to mortgage it.

When the manager insisted on knowing what the money was for, Kate told him she wanted to remodel the house. He lectured her about the struggling housing market and the dangers of mortgaging a house for more than it's worth.

When she'd been able to get a word in edgewise, she'd asked him, "Are you telling me that there's no way I can get any type of loan for that amount of money?"

"That's right, Dr. Chalmet," he'd told her. "It would be virtually impossible, no matter where you went."

So she'd withdrawn the sixty-eight thousand

dollars in her savings account—in cash, despite the manager's disapproving expression.

After leaving the bank, she'd gone to the credit union, but they were less helpful than the bank had been. She'd thanked them and withdrawn the five thousand she had allowed to accumulate in her checking account.

Then she'd gone to her office for a few hours to work on her findings for court, although she wondered whether there was any need for her to continue with her determination of Stamps's state of mind when he'd shot Paul Guillame, now that the kidnapper had decided to target the Delanceys for ransom for their first grandson.

Back at home, she wearily took her cell phone out of her purse and set it on the kitchen counter next to the day's mail, then glanced at her watch. She figured she had about an hour before the kidnapper called. Kate had no idea if seventy-three thousand dollars would be enough to tempt him. She hoped she could tell him it was only part of the payment and she'd be able to get the rest within a week. She had a sinking feeling that he was not going to be impressed with her small offering, given what he might be able to get from the Delanceys, but she had to try. She was desperate. It was her only chance to get her little boy back.

Rubbing her temples, where a headache was starting, she realized she hadn't eaten anything since morning. She opened the refrigerator and stood there, staring at the spaghetti sauce, the fruit and the soft drinks she'd gotten for Travis, but none of it appealed to her. Sighing, she poured herself a glass of milk and picked up the Oreo cookies.

She sat down on a kitchen stool and took one cookie out and twisted the top half off just like she'd shown Max, then used her teeth to scrape the filling off the bottom half. But she had no appetite. She left the two halves sitting on the counter and made herself drink about half of the milk.

For a few seconds she was lost in a memory of Max licking filling off the cookies then dunking them in his milk. Oh, dear God, she missed him so much. Swiping tears off her cheeks, she stood and rinsed her glass. She wished she hadn't sent Travis away. It had been a stupid impulse, fueled by her anger at him for all the things he had done without consulting her. She'd known what he would do—the exact same thing he'd done when she'd told him not to call her again after their one fateful night together five years ago. And he'd done just that—exactly what she'd told him to do.

Why hadn't he refused to leave? Why hadn't

he fought to stay with her? Did he not love her enough to defy her and stay, even if she was stupid enough to tell him to leave?

She set the wet glass on the drain board, and picked up the mail and glanced through it. Nothing but bills and flyers, as usual. When she looked at her watch again, the minute hand had only advanced by nine minutes. She blew out a breath in frustration. She wanted a shower, but she didn't dare take the chance of missing the kidnapper's call. She started pacing. Every time she turned and paced back across the living room toward the kitchen, she eyed the phone and checked her watch. The minutes crawled.

Then, at eleven minutes to seven, the door-bell rang.

"Oh, Travis, don't. Not now. I've got to deal with the kidnapper," she muttered. The bell rang again. She swung it open, prepared to tell Travis that he couldn't come in.

As soon as she turned the knob and pulled on the door, it slammed inward, banging her jaw and her right shoulder. It knocked her back-ward, onto the floor.

A huge man rushed inside and slammed the door shut behind him. Light glinted off a big gun he was holding in both hands. Kate wanted to scream but the blow had knocked the wind out of her and it was all she could do to force small gulps of air past her spasming chest.

The man glanced down at her then turned his attention to her house. He surveyed the kitchen, the living room, and the hallway to the bedrooms and the hall bath.

"Who's here?" he asked, stepping a heavy booted foot on her left hand. He didn't put his weight on that foot, but Kate had no doubt that if he did, her bones would crush like a bird's.

"Noh-nobody," she gasped. With his foot on her hand, she couldn't move. She lay there, on her back on the hardwood floor, still trying to get a full breath and watching him in abject fear. It was the kidnapper.

"Where's your boyfriend?" he growled, digging in his back pocket. He pulled out a set of metal handcuffs and tossed them down on the floor near her. Then he took his boot off her hand. "Put those on."

"Are…you…?"

"Don't talk. Put the cuffs on. Your right wrist first."

She did as he said. The cuff fastened with a loud metallic click. She sat up and started to slip the other cuff around her left wrist.

"Hey!" he yelled. "No. Not in front. In back."

"In back? But—"

"Shut up and just do what I say."

She caught the dangling cuff in her right hand and put her hands behind her back, then tried to slide the cuff onto her left wrist, but she kept fumbling and dropping it. The chain that held the two cuffs together was not very long.

"I can't," she said truthfully. She wished she were smart and brave enough to trick the man by pretending not to be able to fasten the cuffs, but unfortunately, her fumbling was real.

The man spewed out a string of curses. "Don't try anything," he warned. "Do it!"

By some miracle, she managed to get her wrist inside the second cuff and fasten it. It made a flat metallic sound as it locked.

"Now sit over there." He gestured with the gun barrel. "On the floor next to the TV."

Kate went over to the TV and knelt on the floor.

"I said sit."

She rolled sideways, pulling her legs out from under her, then tried to sit up. It was hard with her hands cuffed behind her back. She wiggled around until her back was against the TV cabinet, and watched the man as he disappeared down the hall to search her bedrooms and bathrooms.

As soon as she heard him enter her room, she tried to stand, but again, she was surprised and dismayed at how hard it was to move without the use of her hands. By the time she got to her knees again he was back.

"I told you to sit. What the hell are you doing?"

"I'm sorry," she said. "My hands are falling asleep."

"No, they're not. You haven't had the cuffs on two minutes yet. Stop horsing around or it won't go well for the kid."

With a huge effort, Kate pushed herself to her feet. "Where is Max?" she asked, trying to sound imperious and demanding, but knowing she wasn't pulling it off. "Did you bring him with you?"

"No," he said and laughed shortly. "That's not how it works. You're going with me. I'm going to do this on *my* terms. I'm not about to give you any kind of chance to sic the police or your baby-daddy's family on me." He let his gaze run from her head down her body to her toes and back up again. "So, Doc, how much money were you able to get?"

"A lot," she said eagerly. "You're going to be really happy."

"Where is it?"

She nodded toward the kitchen. "In my purse," she said, swallowing the panic that was pushing its way up her throat. For a man like this, who kidnapped people for a living, was

$73,000 enough? She felt her throat fluttering with the need to scream or run or do something other than just wait pitifully, while this ghoul held the decision of whether or not she could see her child.

"In there?" He looked at her purse, then reached over and picked it up. "It's not very heavy, considering. How much can you have in there. Gotta be less than a hundred thousand, right?" He grabbed her phone from the counter. "We'll take your phone in case I want you to tell your baby-daddy something."

"You're not going to check it?"

"Nope." The man shook his head. "We gotta get out of here. Besides, I'll be able to squeeze five times that out of the kid's grandparents. I'm hoping they'll be willing to pay more for you and the kid together." He gave her the once-over again. "Then again, maybe not."

His flat words and the leer in his gaze chilled Kate to the bone. What had she been thinking, trying to handle this on her own?

He grabbed her arm and pulled her over to the kitchen counter. "Okay. Here's what we're going to do." He unlocked the cuff around her right hand. Then he pulled something out of his shirt pocket, while he picked up the glass she'd left on the drain board. "I want you to swallow this. Here. Get some water."

"What is this?" she demanded, studying the small tablet the kidnapper showed her. She couldn't identify it.

"You don't know? It's a sedative. A very fast-acting one. About five or so minutes after you take it, you'll start feeling really drowsy. You should just go with it. You're not going to get to find out where we're going, anyhow. But if you swallow the pill, you can ride in the back-seat. If you won't, I'm going to put you in the trunk. Do you understand?"

For a brief instant she considered refusing. He'd have to force her out to the car. She could fight and maybe attract attention from the neighbors. Maybe one of them would call the police. But as soon as that thought entered her head, she rejected it. She didn't dare do anything that might put Max in danger. She looked at the tablet in his hand. "I don't want to be drowsy when I see my son," she said. "Can't you just blindfold me?"

He shook his head. "No way. I can't risk someone seeing you with the blindfold on. Now take it or I'll put you in the trunk."

"No, you won't. Somebody might see that, too."

His face flushed. "Then I'll shove the pill down your throat. Nobody'll see that, will they?"

She shook her head. She picked up her glass

and ran some water into it from the tap. She held out her hand and the kidnapper gave her the tablet. She swallowed the tablet.

"Okay," she said. "I swallowed it."

He grabbed her by the back of the neck. "Open up and let me see."

She opened her mouth. He stuck a beefy finger in and swept between her cheeks and gums, the roof of her mouth and under her tongue.

Kate shuddered and did her best not to gag. She didn't quite succeed.

"What?" he demanded, squeezing her neck as he grabbed her jaw in his other hand. He leaned in so close that his face was only about two inches from hers. She swallowed audibly. "You too fancy for the likes of me? You don't like my taste?"

She closed her eyes.

"Open your damn eyes and taste this," he grunted, then put his mouth over hers and kissed her with brutal force. He drew back and grinned at her. "What do you think about that?"

She felt dizzy and her eyes were getting heavy, but she managed to spit at him.

He jerked her backward by her neck, slapped her with his open hand. Then he fastened the handcuffs around her right hand again.

Tears sprang to her eyes.

"Watch out or I might have to really hurt you. Now let's go get in my car. And don't attract any attention. I don't want to shoot anybody and I know you don't want me to."

Despite her fuzzy head and heavy eyes, Kate felt panic gushing up from her throat like an active volcano. She didn't think the kidnapper would shoot anybody in the middle of a quiet neighborhood in daylight, but she couldn't take the chance. She clenched her jaw and let him lead her out to his car. He kept her body close to his to hide the handcuffs from view.

He pushed her into the backseat just about the time the fuzziness covered her brain and her legs decided to give way. He locked the doors with the electronic key, then got into the driver's seat and pressed a couple buttons on the console. "Gotta love child-safety locks." He looked at her in the rearview mirror. "You have a nice nap, now. By the time you wake up, we'll be there."

"I'll get to see Max?"

"If you're good, Doc. If you're good."

TRAVIS GOT TO Kate's house a few minutes after seven. When he pulled into the driveway behind her car, he noticed that all the lights were on, which seemed odd. Kate never left a room without turning off the light—never.

He went up to the front door and knocked. He didn't want to use his key and take the chance of startling her, since she wasn't expecting him. But when she didn't answer after a second knock, he unlocked the door and went inside. Immediately, he knew something was wrong. Her left shoe was on the floor in the living room. He didn't see her purse anywhere, but a glass sat on the kitchen counter. By itself, the glass wasn't a cause for worry, but he saw something streaked on it. He walked over and looked closely at it.

Burning fear ignited at the base of his spine and coursed upward to his scalp. Travis had no doubt what had happened. While he'd been talking to Dawson, the kidnapper had come here and taken Kate. He clenched his fists and closed his eyes. *Focus,* he told himself. Anger didn't accomplish anything. He could hear his sergeant's yell.

Soldiers! Listen up. What's your best weapon? These? He'd held up a rifle and a grenade.

No, sir! the recruits cried.

These? He held up his fists.

No, sir! they cried again.

Then tell me! he bellowed.

A clear and focused mind, sir.

Right now Travis wasn't sure he could clear his mind, much less focus. All he could see was

Kate, terrified and possibly hurt, in the hands of the kidnapper. He should have been here. He should have never allowed her to kick him out. If he'd stood up to her and forced her to listen to Dawson's plan, the kidnapper would never have found her alone.

He flexed his right fist and eyed the wall next to the front door, but he stopped himself. He was reminded of something that Kate had told him, long before he joined the army's Special Forces division.

You don't have to give in to the anger, Travis. It is not stronger than you are.

He'd always given her hell for *psychoanalyzing* him back in college, but now he knew she was right. It had taken him a long time and a lot of specialized training to understand that anger was not only wasted energy, but wasted effect, as well. He had to look at this situation rationally. Kate had been taken by the same kidnapper who held their son. He needed to talk to Dawson and get the rescue operation started. For a few moments, he carefully studied the living room, searching for clues to where the kidnapper had taken her, but found nothing. As he headed for the door, he spotted Max's wooden toy car on the floor next to the couch. Kate had told him the car was Max's favorite. Travis picked it up and put it in his pocket.

From the moment the man had shoved her into the backseat of his car, Kate had been too sleepy to pay attention to anything around her. It seemed to her they'd driven a long way. But she kept drifting in and out of sleep, so she couldn't be sure. At one point she'd roused enough to push herself to a sitting position so she could see out of the windows, but the vehicle's backseat windows had been covered with dark plastic. She tried to look out the windshield, but the brightness of the sun forced her eyes closed and once she closed them, she drifted back to sleep.

Something different in the rhythm of her sleep woke her. She opened her eyes and remembered she was in the kidnapper's car. She had no sense of how much time had passed. "Where are we?" she asked, but the man didn't pay any attention to her. He killed the engine, got out of the car and opened the driver's side rear door.

"Let's go," he said impatiently.

"Where are we?" she repeated.

The man shook his head. "You're mumbling, Doc. I got no idea what you said. Time to get you into the house and into bed, so you can sleep off that sedative. Come on." He wrapped his thick fingers around her upper arm and pulled.

"Ow," she whined. "That hurts." She leaned toward him, trying to take the pressure off her arm. Her eyes were blurry and so was her head. "I need water," she said. "My mouth is so dry."

"Come on, Doc. Try to walk and stop mumbling. I think it's going to be about four or five hours before you can speak clearly. Meanwhile, you need to sleep. They told me the damn pill would last a long time, but I didn't know they meant *hours*." He snaked an arm around her and half carried her toward an old, rusted and peeling mobile home, the kind that could be towed behind a truck.

Squinting, she saw that its far end had been backed into the thick woods and underbrush that surrounded the small trailer park. Her hazy brain couldn't figure out why. If it was supposed to be hidden, it wasn't.

Once she was up the metal steps and at the door, he let go of her. She did her best to stay upright. But when she lifted her head, everything started spinning dizzily and she felt queasy and faint. He opened the door and shoved her inside.

Kate's feet felt too heavy to lift, but with the man behind her pushing, she managed to stay on her feet inside the house. But when he crowded in behind her, she stumbled and almost fell face-first into the orange carpeting.

"Get up!" he growled, then louder, "Shirley? Where are you? Get out here."

Shirley peeked out from a room off the living room through a flimsy aluminum door. "Bent, hush!" she hissed. "Oh," she said when she saw Kate. "You must be Dr. Chalmet."

Kate met her gaze. "Where's my son?" she asked, concentrating on speaking clearly to her.

Shirley poked a thumb backward, in the direction of the tiny bedroom.

Kate tried to move in that direction, but the kidnapper, Bent—or whatever the woman had called him—kept a firm hold on her arm. "Let me go!" she cried, hearing the slurring mumble of her words, almost incomprehensible to her own ears. She jerked her arm but it was no use. All she earned for her effort was the feeling that, if he wanted to, Bent could dislocate her shoulder with almost no effort.

The woman eyed the way Bent was holding her, then crossed her arms and stared at him. "Well?" she asked him.

"What?" he grunted.

"Are you going to let her see the kid?"

At the woman's words, Kate's sluggish mind perked up and she almost cried out. But then a thought occurred to her. If she could keep them thinking that she was overwhelmingly drowsy for a while, maybe she could gain an advantage over them. She did her best to show as little reaction to the thought of being able to see Max, to hold him, as she could.

"Hell, I don't know."

"Come on, Bent. I'm getting sick of being a babysitter. After a while that whining can get to you. Let's lock them in that back room and we can have the bedroom back."

Kate tried to see the man's face by barely opening her eyes to a slit, but when he turned toward her, she closed them again and just stood there, swaying slightly, as if in a stupor.

She felt and heard Bent shift. "She might try to get out the window," he whispered.

"I don't think so," Shirley said. "These bedroom windows are the tiniest windows on the planet, and they're over six feet off the ground. She wouldn't drop the kid that far and she's not going to leave him."

"There's nothing but woods and bushes outside that window, too," Bent agreed. "Hey, Doc," he said to her.

She lifted her chin slightly and opened her eyes as if each lid had a two-pound weight attached to it.

"Wanna see your kid?"

Don't react too much, she warned herself. Slowly she opened her eyes and squinted at him. "Max?" she whispered, letting all the longing that had been building in her for the past two days color her voice. "Max?" She opened her eyes wider. "Where is he?"

"I knew you could wake up if you wanted to." The man's words were so flat and cool that Kate was afraid he was baiting her. That he wasn't going to let her see her son after all.

"Please," she begged.

"Go ahead," he said to the woman. "Put them in that back bedroom. Make sure there's nothing in there she could use as a weapon."

"Way ahead of you, Bent darlin'," the woman said sarcastically. "There's nothing in there but piles of clothes and a stack of empty boxes."

"You're sure?"

"Yeah. Check for yourself if you don't believe me."

"Okay. Get the kid and his stuff. Not the train. That's metal. I don't want her to have anything she could use on the window or on us."

Kate waited, hardly daring to breathe as the woman went into the bedroom. Kate could hear her talking to Max. As heavy as her limbs were from the sedative, Kate had to use all her willpower not to go tearing through the door to her son. She held it together until she heard the woman say, "Honey, want to see your mama?"

Then she heard Max's shriek and she couldn't be still another second. "Max!" she cried and started to run toward the door, but she'd forgotten the kidnapper's hand on her arm. She jerked against his grip.

Then Max appeared in the doorway, his big dark brown eyes wide as saucers, his mouth open in a huge, excited grin. "Mommy!" he shrieked. "Mahmm-eee!" He threw himself at her.

"Maxie," Kate cried and held out her arms and she bent down. Max ran, nearly knocking her over.

"Mommy! You're here!" He wrapped his little arms around her neck and pushed his face into the curve at her neck and shoulder.

"Max," she whispered, pushing her nose into his baby-fine, sweet-smelling hair. For a long time she just crouched there, holding him, reveling in the familiar, sweet smell of her little boy. Then she opened her eyes and met the woman's gaze. She had kept him clean and fed and as happy as he could be without his mommy. Kate gave the woman a nod. Shirley raised an eyebrow and sniffed. She looked away.

"Okay," Bent said. "That's enough. Get up."

Kate closed her eyes again and pressed her nose against her baby's hair.

WHEN TRAVIS GOT to the warehouse, it was after eight o'clock. Ryker was there. He was dressed in a sport coat and tie and was looking at the laptop, where Travis had left Google Maps on the screen. When Ryker saw Travis, he stood and held out his hand. Travis took it and they shook hands.

"Dawson filled me in—" Ryker started, but Travis broke in.

"He's got Kate."

"What?"

"The kidnapper's got Kate," Travis repeated. "He must have gotten there while I was here talking to Dawson. There was a smear of blood on a water glass, so he may have hit her."

"What else did you see?"

"One of her shoes was lying in the middle of the living room. Her purse and phone were gone but today's mail was sitting on the kitchen counter. So she'd been home a little while before he grabbed her."

"Do you think she opened the door to him?" Ryker asked.

A terrible thought occurred to Travis. "He probably rang the bell. She'd have thought it was me."

"So she opened the door without question."

Travis nodded bleakly. "I'm sure she did."

"Okay, so we now have two to rescue."

At that second the door to the warehouse opened and Dawson came in with a young woman dressed all in black. She had midnight-blue hair and about seven or eight gold studs running up and down her left ear, and one long feather earring in her right. She was also wearing black fingerless gloves and black motorcycle boots. Both she and Dawson carried large, hard-sided metal cases.

"Hey, Ryke. Trav. This is Dusty."

Travis was surprised. He probably shouldn't have been, but he'd have sworn he'd heard Dawson refer to his computer wiz as *he*. He nodded to her. She met his gaze and he saw that she had pale gray eyes—they were almost colorless. She nodded back.

"Hi, Dusty," Ryker said. "We met a few years ago when I was helping Dawson on a case."

She nodded at him, then walked over to the table and set the case down on it. She popped the locks and started unloading electronic equipment. Dawson set the other case beside hers and opened it. "I'll leave you to set up the equipment," he said. "We're going to talk strategy."

Dawson pulled a chair to the far side of the long table. Ryker sat in a chair next to him and Travis sat next to Ryker. Just as Dawson opened his mouth, the door opened again and Lucas came in.

Travis had known he was coming, but he still felt self-conscious and embarrassed to face his older brother, after coming back to New Orleans without calling him or anyone else in his family.

"Trav, you son of a gun," Lucas said, grinning.

Travis got up and went to him, holding out his hand. Lucas grabbed it then pulled Travis into a full-on bear hug. Travis gave it right back to him. "Hey, Lucas," he said.

After about thirty seconds, Lucas pushed Travis to arm's length and looked at him. "What the hell happened to you?" he asked. "Last time you were home, you were bulked up like a bodybuilder. You look like you've lost twenty-five pounds."

"Twenty," Travis corrected him. "I had a rough tour."

Lucas nodded and narrowed his gaze. "You were captured," he said, not a question.

Travis waved a hand. "I'm fine," he said. "Let's get started figuring out how to rescue Kate and Max."

"*Kate* and—?" Lucas said.

"Kate and Max?" Dawson spoke over Lucas. "What do you mean, Kate and Max?" he finished.

"When I got to Kate's house this evening, she was gone. Her car was there but her purse and phone weren't. One of her shoes was in the living room and a glass of water had a blood smear on it. She spent all morning and most of the afternoon at the bank and the credit union. I think she was gathering all the cash she could. I don't know if she has savings or got loans, but she told me yesterday that she was taking care of the kidnapper, so I'm sure he called her and she told him she had money."

"Damn," Dawson said on an exhalation.

Lucas used more colorful language.

"Yeah," Travis said. "So what are we going to do?"

Ryker stood and smoothed his tie. "First of all, Travis, I think we need to talk about how we're going to handle this. Reilly's waiting with two off-duty SWAT team members who volunteered to help us out. They're at Airline Highway and U.S. 51, waiting for my signal to go in."

Travis rounded on Ryker. "You're sending a SWAT team in? What are you thinking? You can't do that. My four-year-old son is in there. If half a dozen men storm in, dressed in full

SWAT regalia, how do you think it will affect him?" he demanded. "I'll go. You find the house. I'll get in and rescue them."

Ryker was shaking his head before he finished. "No," he said. "I can't risk sending in a civilian—"

"A civilian?" Travis spat at the same time as Lucas muttered, "Uh-oh."

"Ryke—" Dawson said in a warning voice.

Travis glared at his cousin. "Ryker, I'm an army Special Forces operative. I've had the most specialized training available. I know how to make myself virtually invisible. I can walk through a tangled wood without breaking a twig. I can sneak up on a building set in the middle of an airport runway—no cover anywhere. I can pick any lock. I can break a man's neck with one hand."

"No disrespect, Travis, but you're too close to the situation," Ryker said in a calm but firm voice. "I can't risk you going off half-cocked, or—"

"Ryker," Lucas said. "Hang on a second, if you don't mind."

Travis looked at his older brother. He hadn't expected to see him. The last he'd known, Lucas was still in Dallas, where he'd gone as soon as he'd graduated from high school, declaring he would never again live in the same city as their dad. At some point, somebody was going to have to bring him up to speed on everything that had happened in the Delancey family in the past five years since he'd been gone. But now, his son and the woman he'd driven a thousand miles to see were in danger.

Ryker turned to Lucas. "What is it?" he asked.

But Lucas ignored him. He watched Travis. Travis stood there, holding his gaze, until finally, Lucas cocked his head. "What's different about you, little brother?" he asked.

Travis shrugged. "Five years of training, missions and—difficult situations," he answered.

Lucas shook his head. "You've changed, a lot." He laughed self-consciously. "Don't mean to wax poetic, but you're not carrying around that sullen fury anymore. I can see it in your eyes."

Travis nodded. "All it does is drain your energy and dull your focus."

Lucas nodded again. "That's right. Congratulations. You're smarter than I was at your age." Then he turned to Ryker. "I say let him try. Reilly and his SWAT team can be standing by in case Travis needs them."

It took a while and a long telephone discussion between the twins, Ryker and Reilly, but finally Ryker agreed. "This is unorthodox," he said with more than a touch of irritation in his voice.

"Of course it is, Ryke," Dawson agreed. "Which part of what we've planned *is* orthodox? We're not doing this on the books, so it's already a covert op."

Ryker didn't answer Dawson. He turned to Travis. "Reilly and his team are set up at the U.S. 51 exit off Airline Highway, as I told you earlier. Reilly will communicate with you via a communications device that uses an earpiece and a throat mic, so that no one can overhear either of you. If you get into trouble, say *Mayday* and they'll storm the house."

Dawson stepped up. "Dusty's got the equipment set up. It's time to put everybody in place and get ready to make the call. Remember, we've only got one chance to latch onto that signal—one chance to pinpoint where the kidnapper is keeping Travis's son."

Chapter Ten

By midnight, Travis was in place in a wooded area behind a small mobile-home park located about seven miles from the intersection of U.S. 51 and Airline Highway. When Dawson had called the kidnapper's phone, Dusty had managed to get a GPS location and a tower triangulation that put the kidnapper about two hundred yards from where Travis was standing. Dawson's agent would be flying over in his helicopter in—Travis checked his watch—less than five minutes. If MacEllis Griffin saw the dark green sedan, that would be the final verification that the kidnapper was there.

Travis had the kidnapper's GPS coordinates programmed into his phone and he was ready to go in. All he was waiting for now was for Reilly to get the report from Griffin, then he'd give Travis the okay. The waiting was torture, especially now that he was so close. Kate and their son were less than a football field's length away from him. He wanted more than anything to break in the mobile home's door, take the kidnapper down with a carefully placed blow designed to render him unconscious, then grab Kate and Max and get the hell out of there, leaving the kidnappers for Reilly to handle.

But his training kept him in check. As a Special Forces operative, he understood the need for coordination of effort. The kidnapper was a former cop. He would almost certainly have a weapon. Therefore Travis's team had to consider him armed and dangerous. Since Kate had heard a woman's voice over the phone, the man had a partner who was probably also his girlfriend. But Travis knew that mistakes could cost lives, and he was not about to risk Kate's or his son's lives because he was impatient.

He scanned the area while he waited, making sure he was aware of everything around him. The black blobs that appeared almost shapeless in the dark were mobile homes or RVs. His gaze automatically traced the best path around each of the sad little metal houses on wheels. He didn't know yet which direction he'd take through the cluster of trailers to get to the one holding his family, but he would be ready.

In the distance, he heard the *flap-flap* of helicopter rotors. His heart leaped into his throat. He swallowed against the lump, then took a huge breath. He dug deep inside himself and found the calm focus that had qualified him to be a member of the elite few men who had earned their position in the army's Special Forces.

The helicopter flew over the trailer park slowly and casually, as if it were piloted by a bored traffic cop. Travis touched his ear, which held the tiny bud through which he'd receive the signal to go from Reilly. Within seconds, Reilly's voice, steady and sure, sounded in Travis's ear.

"Vehicle sighted. It's a go. I repeat. It's a go. Golf. Oscar. Leave the channel open. Over."

"Confirmed. On the move. Out," Travis responded.

"Careful, Trav. Out."

Travis moved between the trailers, watching the screen on his phone as the GPS coordinates moved closer and closer to Dusty's mark. He spotted the dark green sedan. It was parked at the end of a dirt path, beside a small trailer that had been pulled so far toward the edge of the parking area that its far end was obscured by woods. When Travis saw that, his pulse gave a small leap. The woods would serve as excellent cover while he ran reconnaissance to map the interior of the trailer and determine where each of the occupants was located.

Behind him, he heard a door open. Instantaneously and without conscious thought, he rolled onto the ground under a shrub. He lay there, still as a rock, as the man who'd opened the door walked outside in his undershirt, boxers and flip-flops. He stretched and yawned, then lit a cigarette and leaned against the side of the trailer, absently scratching himself as he smoked. He finished the cigarette, tossed it on the ground and crushed it with the sole of one flip-flop. Then he yawned again and went back inside.

Travis turned over onto his stomach and crawled silently through the underbrush until he was far enough back in the woods to stand without being spotted. Then he made his careful, quiet way to the trailer. He'd spent some time with Dusty studying the layout of mobile homes of a similar size to this one. From the dimensions and the locations of the small windows, it appeared that the unit had two bedrooms and one bathroom. He circled the unit, noting the position of the front door and comparing it with the layout he'd seen. He made a strategical guess that the second bedroom was the one surrounded by overgrown shrubs and trees. He pulled out a small, powerful pair of binoculars and peered in the largest window. There he saw a man and a woman sitting at a minuscule built-in table. The kidnapper and his partner. He scanned the length of the trailer, but saw no sign of Max or Kate.

Silently, he circled around behind the vehicle and made his way through the vegetation, searching for the window of the room that held his son and the woman he loved.

KATE LAY ON the makeshift bed and held her sleeping child in her arms. During the first part of the night, she'd slept hard—too hard, because of the drug Bent had given her. But a while ago, she didn't know how long, she'd woken up and felt the soft pressure of her little boy's head on her shoulder and heard his sweet, quiet breaths. There was almost no light in the dank little room the kidnapper had put Max and her in. He'd pulled a blanket off the bedraggled couch and tossed it into the room on top of piles of clothes, linens and what looked like trash, then pushed Max and her inside, said, "Keep that kid quiet" and locked the door.

The first thing Kate had done was try to turn on the light, but nothing happened. She'd squinted up and saw that the fixture was empty. The room had one small window that was more than five-and-a-half feet off the floor.

The bottom sill of the window was about at Kate's eye level.

She'd tried to see out the window, but all she'd been able to distinguish were tree limbs and leaves. When Bent had dragged her out of his car and into the trailer, she'd been almost too drowsy to notice anything, but she did recall that the trailer's far end seemed to be nosed into a thick overgrowth of trees and brush.

So she'd lain down with Max, squirmed around to make a comfortable sort of nest, then told him fairy tales until he'd fallen to sleep. She'd kept drifting off during the tales, and Max would touch her face and say, "Mommy? Wake up, Mommy. Finish the story."

Finally, he'd fallen asleep and she'd collapsed into a drug-induced oblivion.

But now she was awake. She bent her head and buried her face in Max's downy hair. He smelled warm and sweet and new, just like a little boy should. Her heart filled so full of love that she wasn't sure her chest could contain it. Her eyes stung with tears and she carefully tightened her hold around his little shoulders. She'd been so afraid she'd never see him again. She had no idea how she was going to rescue him, but she knew one thing. If it meant her life, she would make sure he was safe. Maybe she'd been stupid to deal with the kidnapper on her own. Maybe she'd made the single biggest mistake of her life when she'd sent Travis away, though she could easily analyze why she'd acted the way she had. She'd pushed at him, hoping he'd push back, hoping this time he'd fight to stay with her.

She closed her eyes and took a deep breath, drawing in Max's scent. She'd like to sleep some more. But something intruded into her quest for sleep. A noise, outside the tiny window. Kate held her breath. It was probably a nocturnal animal—a possum or an owl, rustling the underbrush as it hunted for food.

But then she heard it again, a subtle, muffled sound. Kate lifted her head and held her breath. It could be a footstep—a human footstep. Someone from a nearby trailer, taking a midnight walk?

She didn't move for a full minute, expecting to hear the sound again. But when everything remained quiet, she laid her head down on the makeshift pillow she'd fashioned by doubling the corner of the blanket. She'd barely closed her eyes when she heard the noise again.

She shifted, searching for a more comfortable position. A quiet brushing sound, like leaves rubbing across glass, came from the window. Then a knock.

Her head shot up. A knock? Not a brush of

a limb. Not a rustle of underbrush. A knock—like knuckles against the pane.

But no. She shook her head. It must have been a small falling branch that hit the window at just the right angle. It couldn't have been a knock. That wasn't possible.

She relaxed and closed her eyes. The knock sounded again, doubled this time. *Knock-knock.*

Her heart leaped into her throat, lodging there and making it hard for her to breathe. She eased into a sitting position, moving slowly and quietly so as not to wake Max. Whatever was brushing or rapping or pecking against the windowpane, she had to check it out, if only for her own peace of mind. She tiptoed over to the window and, shading her eyes with her hands, peered out through the glass. She saw a large tree limb waving up and down, as if there were something heavy on it. A big possum maybe?

Then she saw a pair of wide, glittering eyes.

Gasping aloud, she threw herself backward so hard she almost lost her balance. She knotted her shirt in her fisted hand and gulped in air, trying to fill her shock-frozen lungs.

What was that? She got her feet under her and stood there for a couple seconds, crouched down below the level of the window. She heard a soft knocking again. The sound made her scalp tighten and tingle with panic.

Something tapped on the window. Kate stayed in her crouch, edging toward the blanket where Max still lay sound asleep, instinctively putting her body between the window and him.

Then a soft thud, followed by a faint screeching sound, like fingernails on the glass, and somehow, the noise of the night was inside the room. She squinted at the window. Could whatever was out there have opened it?

"Kate?"

She started and gasped, half strangling herself and setting off a spate of coughing. She covered her mouth with trembling hands as the spasms overtook her. She coughed as quietly as possible.

"Kate, it's me, Travis."

Her entire body seized in shock. *Travis?* Was she dreaming? With a quick glance down at her sleeping child, she eased toward the window, unsure if she could believe her ears. Had she imagined his voice? Was she inside a dream right now, making up a story of rescue, to compensate for the helpless, hopeless feelings that had engulfed her earlier?

Then she heard a noise that sent paralyzing fear through her. Footsteps on the hollow floor of the trailer. "He's coming," she whispered urgently, still not quite sure whether she was talking to a real person or a dream she'd conjured. The footsteps stopped in front of the door. The knob turned and the door slammed open. When Kate whirled, she was blinded by a bright light. "What the hell?" Bent growled, his voice thick with sleep.

Kate's hands shot up to cover her eyes. Behind her, Max whimpered in his sleep. Thank goodness he slept soundly. She lowered her hands and squinted. She could barely make out Bent's shape in the darkness, but she could see he was holding his gun, with the flashlight propped beneath it. Did she know enough about this man to fabricate an answer that would satisfy him?

"I asked you a question," Bent snapped.

"I wanted some air," she said, trying to sound apologetic and defiant at the same time. "Do you mind if I open the window?" She held her breath. If he decided, on a whim, to accommodate her, he'd see Travis.

He sneered at her. "You think you're fooling me? That's a long way to drop a kid. I wouldn't try it," he growled, brandishing the gun.

She shook her head and opened her mouth to speak, but he cut her off with a curse. "You wake me up again, I'll separate you and the kid. Got that?"

"Mommy?" Max whimpered. His little sing-song voice told her he was 90 percent asleep. She sidled over to the pallet and bent down to pat his back. "It's okay," she whispered.

"I mean it, Doc. Any more noise, and you'll be spending the night in the trunk of the car, and the kid'll have to fend for himself. Got it?"

"Yes," she said.

He shone the flashlight around the room, lighting every corner, every mound of clothing, every shadow. Then he shone the light in her face again, backed out of the room and slammed the door. She heard the lock click.

As his footsteps echoed on the trailer floor, Kate allowed herself a sigh of relief. She patted Max on the back again and bent down close to listen to his breathing. It was steady and even.

Then she crept toward the window. To her shock, she saw a hand—Travis's hand—reach in *through the glass* and unlock the latch on the windowsill. Her pulse was still hammering, and her brain was still cautiously declaring that what she saw could not be true. She kept half her attention focused beyond the small room, to the other end of the trailer.

"Travis?" she asked, so softly that it was barely a whisper.

The hand disappeared and the window raised with a tiny high-pitched whine as the plastic sill strained against the casing. The noise stopped immediately. Then the window started up again, so slowly Kate wasn't sure she actually saw it move. She waited, listening for any noise from inside the trailer.

Finally, moments later, the window was open. "Move away from the window," the voice whispered.

She stepped backward, unable to take her eyes off the black rectangle. Then, as she watched, a pair of long legs in army-green fatigues and boots eased through the opening with almost no sound, followed by a lean upper body in a green fatigue shirt, then dropped to the floor without so much as a quiet thud.

He straightened and looked down at her. "Are you okay?" he whispered. "Is Max?"

It was Travis—solid, strong, real.

"Oh," Kate gasped, so overwhelmed by his presence that she could barely breathe. Then, when she got her first good look at his face, she shook her head in disbelief. He had a black cloth tied tightly around his head and black stripes, smeared like war paint, across each cheek and down his nose. She felt a feeling that was at once nauseating and exhilarating. Her chest was heaving and her head was spinning.

Travis couldn't be here, but he was. She put her hands to her temples and pressed.

"How did you do that?" she asked, gesturing toward the window. She felt as though someone had punched her in the stomach.

He reached out a hand and touched the back of one of hers. "I climbed the tree. That branch was barely long enough for me to reach the window and climb in," he said.

"Trav—" she managed to say, but then her throat totally closed off again and it was all she could do to get air into her straining lungs. "But—the glass. What did you do?" she asked.

"Glass cutter and a suction cup."

Kate frowned.

"I stuck the suction cup on the glass, then cut a circle with the glass cutter. You probably heard the squealing of the cutter. Then I lifted the circle of glass out and reached in to unlock the window."

"Oh," she said, not really taking in everything he said. It didn't matter. He was here.

"Where's Max?" he asked, looking past her. For an instant, her motherly instinct rose up and she had the odd notion that she needed to protect her child from the paint-smeared apparition that stood in front of her. Travis must have felt her stiffen, because he stood still and held out his hands, palms toward her. "I promise I'll do my best not to scare him," he whispered. "But we need to get you both out of here—now."

Kate closed her eyes tightly and willed herself to believe that he was real. Then she held out a hand. He took it in his. She felt his warmth, his strength, his solidity. The lock on her throat released.

"How did you find us?" she murmured and reached up to wrap her arms around his neck. He stiffened at first, but then he must have realized how badly she needed him to hold her, just for a couple seconds.

She tightened her arms around his neck and buried her nose in the hollow of his shoulder, clinging to him as if he were a lifeline in a turbulent ocean. He pressed his cheek against her hair for a few precious seconds. Then he pushed her away.

"We're running out of time," he said, meeting her gaze. A small smile curved his lips. "Are you ready to get out of here?" he asked her.

"You can get us out?"

He placed a hand around the back of her neck and gently pulled her toward him, pressing his lips against her ear. "You bet I can. Now come on. Priority one is getting you and Max out of harm's way. So, what do you need to do to be ready?"

Kate still couldn't quite get control of her emotions. Travis's hand on her neck felt warm and reassuring, but at the same time, it felt iron hard and controlling. She'd never seen this side of him before. He was cloaked in darkness, even down to the black face paint across his cheekbones and nose and forehead. She could barely see him in the dim light that seeped through the brush outside from the other trailers and the moon and stars. But what she saw was a man, a soldier, a warrior.

"I'm ready now," she said.

Travis stared at Kate, his son's mother and the woman he'd always loved. She was exhausted. He could see it in the slump of her shoulders, in the dark circles under her eyes, but she stood straight and tall, ready to do whatever he needed her to do to save her child.

Their child.

He'd hardly dared to look past her at the sleeping boy. He wasn't sure how he was going to react when he came face-to-face with his son for the first time. He had missed so much already. First smile, first laugh, first word, first steps, first tooth. Precious time that he could never recapture. He didn't know much about babies or little boys, but he knew that those four years he'd missed contained a lifetime of irreplaceable firsts. But he had to drag his thoughts back to the moment at hand. He had to get Kate and Max to safety. As he'd told her, that was priority one. Then he'd call Reilly and give him the signal to close in and take the kidnappers.

"Okay," he said roughly, his voice hoarse from emotion. "I'm going to lift you up. You'll grab the top of the window, slide out backward, then drop to the ground. Be prepared. The drop is about five feet, because the trailer is up on blocks. Then I'll pick up Max and lower him out the window to you." He took a step backward and eyed her, head to toe. "Where are your shoes?" he asked, and immediately remembered seeing a high heel on the floor of the living room.

She looked down. "I lost one in the house," she said, "and I kicked the other one off so I could walk. It's okay, Travis. I can do it."

"Walk barefoot through the woods and on the road, carrying Max?"

She lifted her chin and eyed him defiantly. "Yes," she said. "I can do it."

Travis didn't know what he could do. He couldn't give her his boots. They'd just slide right off her feet. He nodded. "Okay," he said. "Let's get started."

"I need to wake him," Kate said, turning toward the sleeping child. "I need to explain who you are and tell him what's going to happen."

"No," Travis said. "He'll be half-asleep and I can have him out the window and into your arms before he wakes up. Will he cry?"

She shook her head. "No. He always wakes up happy. Or at least—" She paused and looked at him. "He did before all this."

"Good." He pulled her close. "Once you have Max, you need to run as fast as you can toward the north."

Kate angled her head and he knew she was trying to figure out which direction was north.

"Listen to me," he said urgently. "When you drop to the ground, you'll be in dense woods, lots of trees and lots of underbrush. You'll be facing the trailer. That's east, okay?"

She nodded.

"Turn ninety degrees to your left. That will be north. Move straight ahead as quietly as you can. There are lots of vines and briars. It's going to be hard without shoes, but push through. Scratches aren't important. Staying alive is. Within about twenty feet you'll be out of the underbrush. Look ahead. Slightly to your right, in the distance, is a tower with red lights on it. Head straight for that tower as fast as you possibly can, carrying Max. You'll see a gas station on the other side of an asphalt road. It's closed and dark. My brother Lucas will meet you there. If he's not there when you get there, you'll find a bathroom on the west side of the station. It's unlocked. Go in there and lock the door from the inside and wait for him. Ask him who he is."

He felt her head shaking side to side. Pulling away, he met her gaze. It was wide and frightened.

"Just stay there?" she said shakily. "In that bathroom? I won't be able to see anything. What if something happens? What if—?"

"Kate, this operation is planned down to the second. Lucas will be there. I will see you in less than two hours, I promise," he said, looking her straight in the eye. "I promise you, Kate. On my life. You can depend on me."

She looked at him for a long time, not blinking, not speaking. Then, slowly, she nodded.

He pressed his lips against her forehead. "Kate," he whispered softly, "I love you."

Her gaze flickered, then met his steadily. "I know you do," she murmured.

But in his head he heard the words she didn't say. *I just don't know if that's enough.*

"Now let's get you out that window."

KATE WAITED, SHIVERING, not with cold but with fear, for Travis to lower Max out the window and into her arms. The tangle of vines, tree branches and underbrush around and under the window was dismaying. She was balanced with one bare foot on a root and the other sank into what felt like a pile of leaves. Her feet already hurt, but like she'd told Travis, she could do it. Max was her number one priority.

Then through the window she heard, "Mommy!"

She jerked. *Oh, no.* Max had woken up when Travis picked him up. Probably, he'd instinctively known that it wasn't his mommy picking him up and he'd woken, seeing Travis's scary, black-streaked face, and panicked.

"Mah—" he cried, stopping in the middle of the word. What had Travis done? She heard scraping and rustling of clothes through the high, small window, then saw Max's head, then his body, come through the window. Travis was holding him with a hand under each arm. She reached up and caught her little boy by the waist as Travis lowered him down. In the distance, she heard footsteps echoing on the hollow trailer floor.

"That's Bent, the kidnapper!" she whispered urgently to Travis. "Let go! I've got Max."

Travis leaned farther out the window. Kate wrapped her arms around her little boy just as Travis let him go. She tightened her embrace and started moving with baby steps toward the north, ducking her head and shielding Max's face with her hand.

"Mah-mee, that soldier gave me my car," he said, his voice a mixture of excitement and fear.

"Run!" Travis whispered.

Kate bent and pushed through the branches, vines and brush as fast as she could. She stumbled when she stepped free of the clinging foliage. Ahead of her were the flashing red lights of the tower. She hiked Max up into her arms and set off at a lumbering jog, the fastest she could go in bare feet while carrying Max.

She wanted to glance back at the trailer so badly. Though she did feel as though the hounds of hell were nipping at her heels, she was desperate to know that Travis was okay. But the foliage was too dense. Even if she looked behind her, she wouldn't be able to see anything.

"Mommy, stop!" Max cried, his little hands fisted around the material of her shirt. He was kicking and squirming. "Mommy!"

"Shh," she whispered. "Shh, Maxie. Don't cry. We're pl-playing hide-and-seek, okay?" she gasped, out of breath. "Shh."

"Hide-and-seek?" Max whispered, then squealed, "Yea!"

She prayed that Travis was okay and that

he'd stopped the kidnapper from following her and Max. She pushed on, slowing down as Max became heavier and squirmed more. "Max, be still. I can't hold on to you."

"Hide now!" he squealed.

She shook him as best she could. "Hush!" she snapped.

Just as he sniffled and opened his mouth to start crying, she heard a sound that ripped through her like heat lightning.

It was a gunshot.

Travis! She stopped and turned. The deep gray sky had turned darker with purple. Soon that predawn darkness would lighten, and neutral gray shadows would change to deep purplish-pink. In the slight glow of dark purple, she saw Shirley, jogging toward them, brandishing something in her hand that caught the pale moonlight like—like steel. It was a gun. And beneath the gun was a large, bright flashlight.

Kate hiked Max higher in her arms and ran, ignoring the stones and gravel and twigs that tore at her bare feet. "Max," she panted. "We're the good guys and they—" she gestured with her head "—they're the bad guys. Stay still so I ca-can outrun them."

To her relief, Max stopped wiggling and

turned backward to watch the woman. "She's catching up, Mommy! Hurry!"

I'm hurrying, she thought, too out of breath to speak. Then she realized she was no longer on the ground. She was on asphalt. *The road.* She blinked and squinted in front of her. There was the gas station. But there was no one waiting to pick them up. She moaned quietly, then tightened her grip on her son. "Maxie, we're almost there," she wheezed. "Al-almost there."

She ran around the left side of the station, praying that Travis was right about the bathroom. He was. Rushing inside, she slammed the door, plunging Max and her from the grayish purple world of early dawn into total blackout.

"Mommy!" Max shrieked when she put him down. Her arm muscles burned like fire as she felt around for a lock. There wasn't a lock on the doorknob, so she ran her fingers up the edge of the door—and touched a metal tube. A chain lock? She felt on the door facing and found a chain. Fumbling, she finally had hold of the clasp on the end of the chain and pushed it into its corresponding hold on the door. *Locked.*

Her wheezing breaths turned into sobs. Behind her, Max was crying.

"Max," she said, "come here." She pulled

him into her arms and held him tightly, hugging him.

"Mommy, it stinks," Max said. "Phew!"

She took a breath and realized that he was right. The bathroom did stink. "That's okay," she muttered. "It stinks, but nobody can get in."

Kate felt around on the dirty, sticky floor, trying to get an idea of how large the room was and what all was in it. She knew that if Shirley figured out where they were, she could shoot through the wooden door. Kate needed something that could serve as a shield. Next to the toilet was a large plastic wrapped case of toilet tissue. It was hardly enough to stop a bullet, but maybe if the slug went through the door, then through the paper, it would slow it down. Then, in the far corner, next to the lavatory, she struck gold. A large metal waste can.

"Max," she said. "Want to play a real game of hide-and-seek?" She had no idea how Max was going to react to the idea of being stuffed into a smelly waste can in a smelly bathroom. But if that's what it took to protect him, then she'd make him do it. By now her eyes had adapted to the dark as much as they were going to. She could see a sliver of light coming in over the door. It wasn't enough light to lend color, or even shape, to most things, but she could see the trash can. She picked it up and emptied the contents on the floor as far into the opposite corner of the room as possible. Then she brushed Max's hair back from his forehead.

"Max, I want you to climb into this can, okay? It's your secret hiding place."

"Mommy, I'm sleepy."

"I know, honey, and you can go to sleep as soon as you're in the ca—the hiding place. Come on. I'll help you in."

"I don't want to," he said firmly. "That's not fun."

She pulled him close. "I want you to hide in there. The bad guys are coming and we have to hide. Now you need to get in the hiding place. Right now. I'll be right behind the can and you can knock and I'll knock back. We can tap out songs on the can—the hiding place. How's that?" She could hear the desperation in her voice. If Shirley kept up the pace she'd been jogging, she'd be across the road any second now.

"Okay, Mommy," Max said, so solemnly that Kate knew he was reacting to her fear and worry. She quickly lifted him into the can. "Now crouch down and get comfortable, okay?" she said.

"Okay," he muttered in a subdued voice.

"I'm right here," she whispered, tapping the side of the can with her knuckles as she maneuvered herself into position in front of the can and held on to her toilet-tissue shield. That put three layers between any bullet Shirley could fire and Max. Dear God, she hoped that would be enough.

Chapter Eleven

Within moments, she heard muffled footsteps. It had to be Shirley, because she hadn't heard a car. Where was Lucas? Kate crouched behind the flimsy toilet-tissue shield.

"Mommy?" Max's small voice ripped into her heart.

"Hey, sweetie," she whispered, reaching around to tap on the can. "Guess what this song is." She tapped out the alphabet song. He didn't answer. "Okay, Maxie, listen." She sang softly. *"A B C D, E F G...H I J K, L M N O P."*

"I'm scared, Mommy," he whined. "Put on a night-light for me."

She had to hold her breath to keep from sobbing out loud as the sound of footsteps on gravel got louder. "Can't right now, Maxie. The bad guys are looking for us. If we want to—" She stopped. *Stay alive.* She couldn't say that to her little boy. "If we want to win, we have to be quiet. Okay?" She tapped quietly on the can and heard his small fingers tapping back.

"El-um-ino-pee," he sang quietly.

"You're so brave, Max," she muttered brokenly. "Just like your daddy."

The crunching footsteps stopped. Kate couldn't tell exactly where the person was, but she knew they were close. Was it Shirley? Was it Lucas? Drawing herself into the smallest ball she could, she held the pack of toilet tissue in front of her and ducked her head.

"Mommy?" Max whimpered quietly. "Too dark, Mommy."

Kate reached behind her and tapped out the "Alphabet Song" on the can and sang in a whisper.

Then she heard the footsteps moving again—closer. They stopped right in front of the door. Kate bit her lip and made herself as small as possible as the knob turned, then rattled.

"Damn it to hell," a muffled voice spat. It was Shirley. An involuntary whimper escaped Kate's throat. She swallowed and held her breath. The knob rattled again, harder. Shirley spewed more curses.

Then—a gunshot split the air. A shock like a lightning strike crackled through Kate's body and she yelped. Behind her, Max let out a squeal, then started sobbing. It took her a few fractions of a second to realize she hadn't been shot. A piece of metal fell onto the floor and rolled bumpily.

The doorknob! The woman had shot the lock. Kate waited, holding her breath, as the bathroom door swung open.

Then, in the distance, more footsteps. Heavy ones.

"Stop!" a male voice ordered. "Stop right there. Police!"

Kate's heart thumped so hard it hurt. Her scalp tightened and her face flushed with adrenaline.

"Son of a—" Shirley growled. Kate could see her through the partially opened door. She pushed the door wide open.

"Ma'am, stop! Don't move!" the policeman shouted. "Drop the gun. Drop it! Now!"

"Mah-mee!" Max cried out behind Kate.

"Drop the gun!" The voice was getting closer. "Drop it now or I'll shoot! Ma'am! Drop it! Drop. It. Now!"

Shirley shot a glance behind her and met Kate's gaze. The woman's eyes were narrowed, calculating. Kate cringed. If she wanted to, Shirley could shoot her.

Then the policeman's shadow fell on Shirley and he had her gun—that quickly. "Now, down on the ground," the cop yelled. "Get down!"

Shirley dropped to the ground in front of the bathroom door. She spread her legs and arms and lay still.

Kate stayed frozen in place, as she watched the cop handcuffing Shirley, dragging her to her feet and hauling her away.

She wondered what she should do now. The policeman had Shirley. It should be safe to come out. But Travis had given her explicit instructions. She was to wait until she knew it was Lucas.

A shadow crossed the doorway again and a knock sounded on the door facing. Kate started and gasped.

"Mommy? Is that the bad guys?" Max cried.

"Dr. Chalmet?" The man stepped into the doorway and paused. Kate stared at him. He was a big man. Tall and broad shouldered, with dark hair. He had a long black rifle in his arms and was dressed in black with what looked like a bulletproof vest across his chest. He didn't exactly look like Travis, but there was a resemblance, in the planes of his face, in his carriage.

"Dr. Chalmet?" he said gently. "I'm Lucas Delancey. Travis's brother. Are you and the boy okay?"

"Oh," she sobbed. "Ye-yes. Yes!" Unwrapping herself from the cramped position, she stood and looked down into the metal trash can. Big dark brown eyes were looking up at her trustingly.

"Come on, Maxie, honey," she said as tears streamed down her face. "The good guys won."

Picking him up, feeling his arms wrap around her neck and his legs circle her waist, she could no longer hold back. She burst into tears.

Behind her, Lucas said, "Is there anything I can do? I can hold him for a minute if you want. Are either of you injured?"

She shook her head, trying to get her sobs under control. She had her nose buried in Max's hair. Sniffling, she lifted her head. "We're fine. Where's Travis?" she asked.

"I haven't heard anything from Reilly, which is a good sign," he said.

"I heard a gunshot inside the trailer while we were running away."

Lucas was still studying her. "Are you sure you're all right? Your feet are bleeding and you're covered with scratches," he said. "Come on. Let's put you in the front seat of the car. We're going to have to go to the local police station. I've got to deliver my unexpected prisoner there." He gestured. "I guess you know who she is." He gestured toward a black car. Shirley was in the backseat, her hands cuffed behind her, looking sullen.

"Her name's Shirley. She's the kidnapper's girlfriend," Kate said. "But I don't understand. What was she doing? She shot the lock off the bathroom door. She could have shot us or taken us hostage but all she did was look at me."

Lucas shrugged. "I don't think she realized y'all were in there. I think she wanted to use the bathroom as a hiding place for herself." He opened the passenger door.

"This is false arrest!" Shirley cried as soon as the door was open. "You're going to be in big trouble for assaulting me. I got rights."

Lucas stuck his head in. "If you don't shut up, I'm going to tape your mouth. Got that right," he said conversationally.

Shirley spewed a few choice words then went silent.

Kate climbed into the passenger seat awkwardly, still holding Max. "Maxie, honey. Let go of my neck. We're just fine. Sit on my lap, sweetie." He wiggled, but he was too sleepy to do anything but whimper.

Lucas got into the driver's side of the car. "The station's not far. Put your seat belt on and hold on to Max. I'll drive slowly." He started the car and drove out of the gas station parking lot and onto the road. The sky was beginning to turn pink and blue and there was a fresh morning smell to the air.

"I've got to warn you," he said. "I know it's been a long, frightening night for you and Max, but I'm afraid your ordeal isn't over. The local cops have no idea what's been going on. So, be prepared, because you're going to have a long, harrowing day."

"I've been through the longest, most awful five days of my life. But I have my son back now. Believe me, compared to what we've been through, this day will be a picnic." She got the seat belt fastened and wrapped her arms around Max. He was asleep, for which she was grateful.

Lucas's cell phone rang.

"Please," Kate said quickly. "Ask about Travis."

A snort sounded from the backseat. "Travis. That your boyfriend's name?" Shirley said. "Good luck, 'cause last I saw of him, he was lying in a puddle of his own blood outside that window. Bent shot him."

WITHIN THE EIGHT minutes it took to get to the St. John's Parish Sheriff's Department, Lucas had gotten in touch with Ryker, who told him that Reilly and his men had taken Bentley Woods into custody and had rushed Travis to River Parishes Hospital, less than two miles from the sheriff's office. Kate was relieved that he was at the hospital, but it worried her that nobody had any word about his condition.

She watched as Lucas patiently explained the whole situation to the sergeant in charge on the midnight shift, who stared at him drowsily. Once Lucas had finished, the sergeant looked at him blankly for a second, then told him he needed to talk to the sheriff.

Because she had Max, Kate was allowed to wait in the break room, which had an old leather couch in it. She got Max settled down on the couch with a blanket over him and his little wooden car clutched in his hands. Then she crossed to the counter where a coffeepot sat, it's On light beckoning her. The coffee didn't smell great, but she poured herself a cup anyhow. It wasn't the coffee's taste she was after, it was the caffeine. She didn't want to fall asleep because she knew if she did, she'd feel lousy when she woke up. She figured it would be better to stay awake.

SHE'D LEARNED A lot listening to Lucas's recounting of the situation to the sergeant. Travis had told her that Dawson and his computer whiz kid were working on a way to pinpoint the exact location of the kidnappers through his cell phone. She knew that they'd only had one chance, because as soon as Bentley

Woods answered his phone and realized the caller wasn't who he was expecting, he'd hang up. She hadn't known that Travis had found Woods's phone number in Congressman Whitley's phone. That meant Whitley was a party to the kidnapping.

Lucas also told the sergeant that Stamps was apparently unaware of the kidnapping scheme aimed at saving him from a felony conviction, but that there was suspicion, if not actual evidence, that Darby Sills was involved.

The sergeant was unhappy that the sheriff's office hadn't been brought in on the ambush from the beginning, and let Lucas know in no uncertain terms what he, and by extension the sheriff, thought about a bunch of cowboys from the NOPD and the St. Tammany Parish Sheriff's Department pulling off a dangerous, harebrained scheme like that right under the St. John's sheriff's nose. Lucas was appropriately apologetic and earnest about their fear for the child's life if they brought in any official authorities. He was careful to explain to the sergeant that a professional kidnapper, a disgraced dirty cop named Bentley Woods, had been called in from Chicago to handle the job. Through a connection of his own in Chicago, Lucas had learned that Woods had been a prime suspect in a couple murders for hire in

Cook County, Illinois, but that in neither case was there enough evidence to convict him.

That information horrified Kate. Her child had been in the hands of a man who committed murder for money. She moved to the couch and draped her arm across Max's legs in a protective gesture, trying to shove the image of the kidnapper with that gun in his hand out of her brain.

After about forty minutes, the sheriff came in, and nodded for Lucas and the sergeant to follow him into his office. He closed the door.

Kate couldn't hear anymore, and despite the coffee, she could barely keep her eyes open, so she decided to catch a nap while she was waiting. She laid her head back against the couch cushions and dozed.

"Dr. Chalmet?" a voice said.

Kate cringed as she opened her eyes. For a split second her drowsy brain told her that it was the kidnapper talking to her, before she woke up enough to remember that she was in a room at the Sheriff's Department of St. John the Baptist Parish.

She looked up. It was a man in a long-sleeved shirt with the sleeves rolled up. He was youngish, maybe late thirties, but had the look of a chronically tired suburban dad. "Dr. Chalmet? I'm Detective Adrian Darrow. I need to ask you some questions." He gestured to the wooden table, where a couple fast-food bags and a small recorder sat. "I got a chicken biscuit, a sausage biscuit and some French toast sticks. Plus some milk and orange juice. I hope that's okay."

"Thank you," Kate said, glancing at Max. "I think Max is going to sleep for another couple hours—he's exhausted. But the sausage biscuit and the orange juice sound great."

He pushed the bags toward her.

"What time is it, anyway?" Kate asked.

"About a quarter to nine," he said.

"Wow. It was just after sunrise when we got here," she said, then took a bite of the sandwich. "Good," she mumbled, chewing. Once she'd swallowed, she asked, "Is there any information about Travis Delancey? He was shot. They took him to the hospital that's close to here, I think."

"I don't know," Darrow said. "I'll get somebody to check. But first, I need to ask you some questions." He turned on the recorder. Kate spent the next two hours reliving all the fear and anxiety of the past five days as she answered his questions.

"I DON'T CARE who I have to see, how sore I'm going to be or how many forms I have to sign if I leave now. Do you understand?" Travis groused. "It's after noon. I've been here since before dawn and I am leaving—with or without discharge orders."

The nurse opened her mouth, closed it, opened it one more time, then whirled on her heel and left the room.

Travis turned and looked at his brother Lucas. "Don't just stand there. Help me."

Lucas laughed. "That dead-calm look you gave the nurse. Is that some supersecret, classified U.S. throat-paralyzing glare?"

Travis gave a half shrug and kicked the sheet off his right leg. He wiggled it sideways until his foot was hanging off the bed. Then he braced his hands on the guardrails of the bed and lifted his butt and twisted to the right. When he lowered himself back down, he groaned.

Lucas laughed some more.

"Luke, I swear I'll come up off this bed and beat you into next week."

"No, you won't," Lucas said. "You can't even stand up. I can't believe a bullet to the butt cheek is all it took to ground you."

"Shut up and help me get up. I need to see Kate and my son."

Lucas's grin faded. "Okay. I know. But while you're dressing, we need to talk."

Travis had known this was coming from the

moment he'd first seen his brother in Dawson's warehouse.

"A Dr. Gingosian called Mom and Dad."

Lucas's words almost knocked Travis flat in the bed. Packed into that one sentence were five years of surprises. "I figured he'd call eventually. Where's doctor-patient confidentiality when you need it?"

"Maybe the Hippocratic oath takes precedence. He told them what happened to you and said you might need psychiatric care."

Travis set his jaw and blew out a frustrated breath. "I don't. What I need is to see that Kate and Max are all right."

"You need to go see the folks."

"This, from you?" Travis responded. "First, you're calling 'em *Mom and Dad.* Seems like the last time I heard you call him Dad was— let me think—oh, yeah. Never! He was always *that bastard* or if you were feeling sentimental, *the old man.* And what's up with you being back here? When you took off for Dallas, you said you'd never come back."

"Yeah, well, things change. But we were talking about you."

"No, we weren't. What things changed?"

"I got a call from Brad Grayson. Remember him? He was afraid his younger sister,

Angela, was in danger, because of a case he was trying."

"Brad and Angela. I do remember them. She always wanted to follow you guys around."

"Yeah." Lucas smiled. "Brad asked me to bodyguard her without her knowing it. Turns out Brad was right. The guy he was prosecuting sent some thugs after her, hoping to use her to force Brad to throw the trial. It took some doing but we finally ended up catching the thugs and keeping Ange safe. Now Ange and I are—" He held up his left hand and Travis saw the gold wedding band on his third finger.

"No way!" he said. "Married? You and Dawson both? Did all the Delancey grandkids get married while I was gone?"

"Well, Ryker and Reilly did. Oh, and Rosemary."

"Rosemary?" Travis's head was spinning, trying to take everything in. "But she's—?"

Lucas shook his head. "Nope. She's not dead. Turns out she survived that attack in her apartment all those years ago. An old woman who owned a little voodoo shop on Prytania took her in and saved her life. She was living that close to us for all those years. Detective Dixon Lloyd, Ethan's partner, found her. She has traumatic amnesia, but she's slowly getting her memories back."

Travis laughed shortly. "Looks like I've got a lot of congratulating to do and wedding gifts to buy. Man, sounds like the family started its own soap opera while I was gone."

"Started?" Lucas echoed. "The Delancey clan has always had a flair for the dramatic."

"Well, that's true. So, anything else I need to know? How are Ethan and Cara Lynn? I already heard about Harte from Kate. Maybe I won't miss his wedding."

"Our baby brother grew up fast," Lucas said, smiling. "Ethan and Cara Lynn are doing good. They've both managed to avoid the marriage bug so far."

Just as he finished speaking, the door opened and a young man in scrubs stepped into the room. "Mr. Delancey? I understand you're ready to leave."

"That's right. Can I go now?"

"The discharge orders are written. You need to come back here or follow up with your personal physician to have those stitches out in about five days. No longer than that."

Travis nodded impatiently. "Got it."

"I've written you a prescription for pain, in case you need it." He held out a slip of paper.

Travis took it without looking at it. "I won't."

The young doctor turned to Lucas. "I understand you're with NOPD?"

Lucas nodded.

"I'm sure you know the St. John's Parish Sheriff's Department wants to see Mr. Delancey. The sheriff asked me to remind you of that."

Lucas nodded and thanked him. As he left, Travis again lifted himself off the bed with his arms, turned his torso toward the side and lowered himself with a groan. "A little help here?" he said through gritted teeth.

"Fine," Lucas said and gave him a hand. With help from his brother, Travis got up, dressed and went to St. John's Sheriff's Department. But by the time he got there, Kate was gone and the sheriff was waiting for him. He was subjected to over two hours of questioning.

As soon as they were done with him, Lucas appeared.

"Nobody'll tell me anything about Stamps and Whitley and Sills," Travis said.

Lucas propped a hip on the edge of a desk. "Whitley was picked up for questioning in Baton Rouge. They'll be talking with the sheriff's office here. Stamps still denies knowing anything about the kidnapping and Sills is acting as though we've accused him of high treason. He's incensed that anyone would think he'd stoop so low."

"Well, that tells me almost nothing."

"It sounds like Whitley's going to take the fall and Sills and Stamps just might walk."

Travis glared at his big brother. "Think you could use some of your influence to get them to let me go now?"

"I already did. I told the sheriff your butt hurt."

"Oh, ha-ha," Travis said. "Take me to Kate's house."

"When are you going to see the folks?"

"When I'm done meeting my son and talking to my—to Kate."

Chapter Twelve

It was almost seven o'clock on Saturday evening when Travis knocked on the door to Kate's house. He still had the key she'd given him but he didn't want to walk in on her. He had an overpowering sense of déjà vu. Here he was, standing outside her door with no idea of what he was going to say when she opened it, just like five days ago.

Five days ago. In one sense, he couldn't believe it had been that long. In another, it had seemed as if everything that had happened couldn't fit into a month.

He shifted, sending searing pain through his hip, because in truth, the bullet had lodged in his gluteus minimus muscle, not the gluteus maximus. Fat lot of good that difference would mean to his brothers and cousins. He'd already had just about all the kidding he could take.

The doorknob turned and he stiffened and grimaced.

Kate opened the door about four inches and

peered out at him. She didn't say anything. She had on the terry-cloth robe and her hair was damp and her feet were bare. Her eyes were tired looking and red, but he stared at her, thinking she was the most beautiful thing he'd ever seen.

"Kate," he said. "I wanted—" Suddenly he was tongue-tied. What he really wanted, he couldn't say—not to her. He could hardly admit it to himself. He wanted to meet his son, certainly. He'd barely had a chance to look at Max, much less talk to him. But he knew that what kind of relationship he had with him was 100 percent Kate's call. He didn't deserve anything, so whatever she wanted to grant him, he would take and be grateful for it.

But that wasn't what had tongue-tied him.

Kate turned her head to glance behind her at her son. Then she said, "You wanted—?"

His mouth felt dry as a desert. "May I see Max?"

She pressed her lips together until they turned white at the corners. Then she lifted her chin and looked at him with a direct, unblinking gaze. Finally, she blinked slowly and nodded. "Okay, but he's had his bath and he's very sleepy. I doubt he'll be able to stay awake for another half hour."

Travis swallowed and nodded. "I won't stay long."

She stepped backward and swung the door

wide. He stepped inside, doing his best not to limp. He saw Max in the living room on the floor, playing with his wooden car.

Travis felt Kate's eyes on him. He angled his head toward her without taking his eyes off his son. "Thank you," he said, his voice hitching, then, "Hi, Max. How're you doing?"

His son looked up, his wide eyes the same shape as his mother's, but with dark brown pupils. *Like mine,* Travis thought. "What you got there? Is that your favorite car?"

Max stared at him for a moment, then nodded. "I remember you," he said. "You gave it to me when you handed me out the window. Your face was painted like a soldier."

Travis glanced at Kate, whose mouth quirked slightly as she gave him a tiny, awed shake of her head. "He's a pretty smart kid," she whispered.

"That's right, Max. It was me."

"Are you a soldier?"

Travis walked around the couch and gingerly sat on the coffee table. "I am. How do you know about soldiers?"

"I see them on the TV. Some of them use paint on their faces. I was scared, but I figured out you were on our side."

"I see." Travis was stunned. Max was not

just smart, he was scary smart. "I think you take after your mom."

Max nodded, as if he heard that every day. "Did you just come home?" he asked.

That rendered Travis speechless. He turned and looked at Kate, silently asking for help. What did Max mean, *come home?*

"Max?" Kate said. "What do you mean?"

"You know, Mommy. Like heroes on TV. They come home and their family is there and the TV is there, then the soldiers are heroes."

"Oh." Kate sounded dumbfounded, too. Travis sat there as Max looked at his mom, then at Travis, then back to his mom.

"Well, yes," Kate finally said. "He is a hero. He saved you and me, right? When he helped us out the window." She came over to the coffee table and sat next to Travis. "Max, come here a minute."

Dutifully, Max got up from the floor and went to his mom. She picked him up and sat him on her knee, then looked at him closely. "Are you sleepy?" she asked.

"Uh-uh," Max said, shaking his head. "I mean, no, ma'am."

"Okay." Kate looked at Travis with an unreadable expression on her face.

Travis looked back, frowning. What was she about to do? Take him away and put him to bed?

She inhaled deeply. "Okay," she said again on a sigh. "Max, you know how you sometimes ask me about your daddy?"

"Uh-huh," Max said, rolling the car up her arm. Kate stopped it with her hand.

"Max, listen to me a minute. Tell Travis what I've told you about your daddy."

Max pouted a little but he finally answered. "My daddy is a soldier. He's protecting the United States. He—um—"

"He doesn't live with us—" Kate prompted.

Travis heard a slight break in her voice.

"He doesn't live with us but he's a good man. He's a—" Max looked thoughtful for a second, then gasped. "Mommy!" His face lit up and he beamed at his mom. Then he turned his attention to Travis. "You don't live with us and you're a hero! Does that mean you're my daddy?"

Travis felt hot tears sting the backs of his eyes. He couldn't speak. A lump the size of Louisiana was suddenly blocking his throat. His hazy gaze turned toward Kate.

"Well, soldier?" she said, her voice quavering.

"Wh-what should I say?" Travis muttered.

"It's up to you," she said. "But if you were telling me the truth the other day when you said you would never leave me alone again, then maybe you should tell your son the truth, too."

"I'm—" Travis began, but that lump was still there. He tried again. "I'm your daddy, Max," he said gruffly. "Is that okay with you?"

Suddenly, Max's eyes got wide and he looked unsure of himself. "Mommy?" he said in a small voice. "It's okay, right?"

Kate pulled him close and kissed his face over and over, until he squealed. "Sweetheart, you're awfully young to be as wise as you are. But yes. Your daddy is a hero and a soldier and he's sitting right here in front of you." She took a shaky breath, glanced sidelong at Travis, then said, "He's been hurt and he's going to have to have some help getting better." She glanced at Travis again. "But we just might end up being a family together. Would you like that?"

Max looked at her for a moment. Then he turned and looked at Travis.

Travis smiled and winked at him, and Max hid his head in the curve of his mom's shoulder.

"Max? What do you say?" Kate asked him.

Travis couldn't breathe. He'd faced enemy fire. He'd faced captivity, severe hunger, cold and darkness. He'd faced beatings and torture. But nothing had ever scared him as much as waiting for this little boy's answer did.

Then Max nodded, his head still buried in Kate's shoulder. "Yes, ma'am," he said. "Wait till I tell Justin and Marcus that my daddy's a hero."

Epilogue

Dr. Kate Chalmet was nervous as a cat. She had to go to Robert and Betty Carole Delancey's home to attend a Memorial Day cookout by herself. Travis had been gone for the past three days to Walter Reed National Military Medical Center, then to Washington, D.C., to receive his medical discharge. His plane was due to land at six o'clock. Lucas was picking him up at the airport.

Kate parked in front of the sprawling white house in Chef Voleur, Louisiana, on the north shore of Lake Pontchartrain. She exited and opened the back driver's side door to let Max out of his car seat. He was halfway done with the fastenings by the time she opened the door.

"Max, I've told you before, don't start undoing the belts until I stop the car."

"I didn't, Mommy. I'm fast."

Kate laughed. "You sure are, and getting faster every day."

"Kate!" a pleasant, lilting voice called.

Kate finished undoing Max's seat belts and he jumped out of the car. "Stay with me, Max. Hi, Cara Lynn." Kate held out her arms and Cara Lynn and she hugged. "It's been a long time."

"Too long," Cara Lynn agreed. "Max, come here," she said. "I've got something for you."

"For me?" Max exclaimed. "Yea! What is it?"

Cara Lynn handed him a small paper bag. "See for yourself."

"Mommy, it's an LSU baseball cap. It's your school, right?"

"That's right." Kate smiled at Cara Lynn. "Too cute. Thanks."

Cara Lynn was looking at Max, shaking her head. "I can't believe I didn't see it from the beginning. Even as a newborn he had that hair and those eyelashes. He's just like Travis—looks and actions. Look at him. My first nephew! Why didn't you tell me?"

"I'm sorry," Kate said. "I guess I was afraid of what you would think. And now I'm terrified of what your folks are going to say."

Cara Lynn gestured for Kate to walk with her up the long curving sidewalk. "Don't be. Mom's sweet. She'll adore you just because you've brought her a grandson. Then when she gets to know you, you'll be just like one of the family."

"And your dad?" Kate asked apprehensively.

"Dad talks pretty well. But he doesn't interact with anyone much. I have no idea what he'll think about Max. I do know that Lucas and Ethan—and I'm sure Travis—will be watching him closely. They don't have good memories of him from their childhood."

"But he won't—"

Cara Lynn's lips thinned. "His stroke was massive. He can barely move and talk. He's not going to hurt your son."

Kate's face burned. "I'm sorry, Cara. I didn't mean—"

She waved a hand. "It's okay. I get mad at my older brothers a lot. Harte and I don't remember Dad the same way they do. The man we grew up with wouldn't—couldn't hurt a fly." She walked up to the door and swung it open. "Come in," she said to Kate. "And brace yourself. You're about to meet the entire Delancey clan."

Kate held Max as Cara led her toward a pretty woman and a man in a wheelchair.

"Mom, Dad, this is Kate Chalmet."

Kate smiled shakily and clutched Max more tightly as she waited to see what Travis's parents would do.

"Kate," Betty Carole Delancey said. "I'm so glad to meet you. And this must be Max."

Max ducked his head and hid his face in Kate's blouse. "Max," Kate said. "This is Travis's mother."

"Now, Kate," Betty Carole said in an admonishing tone.

Kate cringed, but before she had a chance to wonder what she'd said wrong, Travis's mother continued.

"Max, I'm your grandmama. What do you think about that?"

Max peered at her sidelong. She grinned at him and finally, he lifted his head and smiled at her. "Grandmama?" he said.

Betty Carole laughed. "Yes. That's right. And this is your granddaddy." Betty Carole turned to Robert Delancey, who was eyeing Max with a pensive expression on his face. "Robert, this is Max. He's Travis's son."

"Travis," Robert said, his mouth twisting a little as he worked to form the word.

Max's fist tightened on the back of Kate's shirt. "Mommy?" he whispered.

"It's okay, Max," she said. "He's your granddaddy."

Betty Carole placed a hand on Robert's shoulder. "Robert, where's Travis's car?" she asked him, then looked at Max. "Your granddaddy wanted me to find a special toy car that Travis had when he was a little boy. Would you like to see it?"

"Car?" Max echoed, peering at her and then at Robert.

Robert nodded. "Car—" he said. "Max. You want—car?"

The little boy nodded. "Let me down, Mommy."

Kate set him on the floor and he stood there, watching Robert as the older man reached under the blanket that covered his legs and came out with a red wooden car. It was old, and the paint was scratched and dinged, but as soon as Max saw it, he reached for it.

"Mommy! It's like mine!" he cried.

Robert looked up at her. "Okay?" he asked.

She nodded, smiling.

"Okay." Robert held out the car and Max took it.

"Max," Kate said. "What do you say?"

Max looked at Robert. "Thank you," he said. "Granddaddy."

"Oh," Betty Carole exclaimed quietly. When she looked at Kate, there were tears in her eyes.

Kate felt her own eyes sting. "Thank you both," she murmured.

At that instant, Dawson approached and introduced Kate to his wife, Juliana. They asked permission to show Max a computer football game.

Then Betty Carole introduced her to Lucas's wife, Angela, a dark-haired beauty who seemed perfectly at ease in the middle of dozens of Delanceys. Ethan, who was younger than Lucas and Travis, seemed more serious and intense than his brothers. Harte greeted her warmly, introduced her to Danielle, then took her across the room to meet his aunt and uncle, Michael and Edina Delancey.

Dawson's brothers, Ryker and Reilly, the twins she'd heard about, were there. Ryker told her that his wife, Nicole, a chef, was helping with the meal and that he didn't know where Reilly's wife, Christy, was. "She's probably in the den, playing with Max and Dawson," he said with a smile.

Then Edina brought over a red-haired woman. She introduced her as Rosemary Delancey. "This is my daughter," Edina said. "She has just come back to us after twelve years. We thought she was dead. And this is her fiancé, Detective Dixon Lloyd." Kate was nearly dumbfounded. Even with the faint scar that ran from her hairline to her jaw, Rosemary was stunning, her long wavy hair pulled back at her nape. She and Dixon were a study in contrasts. He was intense and darkly handsome, and he only had eyes for her.

Kate heard Travis's voice behind her. She turned and saw him standing inside the front door with Lucas. The two of them were talking with Paul Guillame. Kate excused herself and stepped closer. She heard a snippet of their conversation.

"Well, I should think not," Paul was saying. "Senator Stamps was shocked to find out what Gavin Whitley had done."

Lucas's lip curled in faint derision. "And Darby Sills was clueless, as well, I guess."

Paul waved a hand. "I think Darby Sills could fall into a pigpen and come out smelling like a rose. I'm just glad that the D.A. dropped the charges against Myron. He didn't have to face prison or have to live with the stigma of being declared temporarily insane. Now the D.A. has Whitley's huge kidnapping case to sink his claws into."

Travis pulled Kate close when she walked up. "Well, Whitley and Woods and Shirley Hixon will all pay for their parts in the kidnapping."

Kate nodded. "And Max is okay."

"Oh," Paul said. "Did you all hear? Claire is coming home."

Travis said, "Aunt Claire? Why? I thought

she was perfectly happy in Paris with— What was his name? The superwealthy French guy?"

"Oh, for goodness' sake," Paul said. "It's Ektor Petrakis, the superwealthy *Greek* guy. And in fact, that is why she's coming home. Ektor died."

"Oh," Travis said. "Sorry to hear that."

"Yes, well, I never understood what she saw in him that would make her leave her family," Paul continued. "I'll be so glad to see her. She's in her late seventies now, you know."

Lucas excused himself. Travis started to introduce Kate to Paul, but he waved a hand. "Yes, yes, Kate. We met the other day when she interviewed me. Oh! There's that lovely Rosemary. I need to speak to her. Later." And he was gone.

Kate turned to Travis, shaking her head. "I'm not sure I've ever seen a family this large—anywhere. How do you keep up?"

He laughed. "It's a sort of comfortable chaos. It's been like this all my life." He kissed her lightly on the lips.

"What did the doctors say?" she asked him.

A look of annoyance crossed his face. "I have to see a shrink for a few months, to be sure I've fully recovered from my traumatic experience," he said wryly.

"No, I meant about your—wound," Kate said, grinning. "Your *posterior* wound."

"All right. I get enough ribbing from the guys. I'm not going to take it from you, too," Travis said, trying not to smile. "So, the shrink thing. I don't guess I can see you?"

"No," Kate said, "but I can recommend someone." She touched his cheek. "How are you?"

He smiled at her. "I'm good. Really good. Where's my son?"

"He's in the—" she gestured vaguely "—one of the rooms, playing with Dawson. You'd better watch that guy. He seems to be a Pied Piper around kids."

"Yeah, he always was." Travis turned his head and whispered in Kate's ear. "So how are you doing?"

"Totally overwhelmed by your family. Didn't you tell me none of your siblings or cousins were married when you joined the army five years ago?"

"Yeah," Travis said on a laugh. "I've been trying to count the fallen ones."

"Here's my best guess," she said. "All four of Michael's children—Dawson, the twins, Ryker and Reilly, are married or soon to be, with Rosemary's engagement to Detective Lloyd. In your family, Lucas is married. From what everyone is saying, Harte and Dani are about to be married, and—"

"And what?"

Kate, suddenly at a loss for words, just shrugged.

"And if we get married that'll be seven out of nine, right? Leaving only Ethan and Cara Lynn."

She nodded, her cheeks pink.

Travis slid his arm around her waist and whispered, "What do you say we find one of the unoccupied rooms on the second floor and go *discuss* our options."

At that moment, Betty Carole called out, "Everyone? Everyone! Dinner's ready. Come and taste Nicole's creations. She has done a superb job."

"I think I'd better start learning how to get along with your huge family, Travis Delancey."

"Mommy!"

Kate turned in time to be pummeled with an armful of a four-year-old. Travis stooped and swept up Max before he could knock her down.

"Watch it, little man. Where do you think you're going?"

Max looked at Travis, at Kate, then back to Travis. "These people are all yours?" he asked.

Travis put a hand on Max's head. "They're all mine—and they're yours now."

"Ours," Max said. "This is a big family."

"Very big," Kate agreed.

"There's lots of little families in big families."

Kate met Travis's eye. "Told you he was smart," she mouthed.

"We're a little family, right?" he demanded, tapping his mommy's face. "You and me and my hero daddy?"

Travis realized the entire roomful of people were watching them. Then, as if someone had waved a baton, they all went silent, waiting for Travis to answer his son.

Travis looked at Kate. She stepped up to him and slid her arm around his waist and laid her head on his shoulder. "We are definitely a little family, Max," she said.

* * * * *

LARGER-PRINT BOOKS!
GET 2 FREE LARGER-PRINT NOVELS PLUS
2 FREE GIFTS!

HARLEQUIN®

INTRIGUE®

BREATHTAKING ROMANTIC SUSPENSE

YES! Please send me 2 FREE LARGER-PRINT Harlequin Intrigue® novels and my 2 FREE gifts (gifts are worth about $10). After receiving them, if I don't wish to receive any more books, I can return the shipping statement marked "cancel." If I don't cancel, I will receive 6 brand-new novels every month and be billed just $5.49 per book in the U.S. or $5.99 per book in Canada. That's a saving of at least 13% off the cover price! It's quite a bargain! Shipping and handling is just 50¢ per book in the U.S. and 75¢ per book in Canada.* I understand that accepting the 2 free books and gifts places me under no obligation to buy anything. I can always return a shipment and cancel at any time. Even if I never buy another book, the two free books and gifts are mine to keep forever.

199/399 HDN F42Y

Name _____ (PLEASE PRINT) _____

Address _____ Apt. # _____

City _____ State/Prov. _____ Zip/Postal Code _____

Signature (if under 18, a parent or guardian must sign) _____

Mail to the **Harlequin® Reader Service:**
IN U.S.A.: P.O. Box 1867, Buffalo, NY 14240-1867
IN CANADA: P.O. Box 609, Fort Erie, Ontario L2A 5X3

Are you a subscriber to Harlequin Intrigue books
and want to receive the larger-print edition?
Call 1-800-873-8635 today or visit www.ReaderService.com.

* Terms and prices subject to change without notice. Prices do not include applicable taxes. Sales tax applicable in N.Y. Canadian residents will be charged applicable taxes. Offer not valid in Quebec. This offer is limited to one order per household. Not valid for current subscribers to Harlequin Intrigue Larger-Print books. All orders subject to credit approval. Credit or debit balances in a customer's account(s) may be offset by any other outstanding balance owed by or to the customer. Please allow 4 to 6 weeks for delivery. Offer available while quantities last.

Your Privacy—The Harlequin® Reader Service is committed to protecting your privacy. Our Privacy Policy is available online at www.ReaderService.com or upon request from the Harlequin Reader Service.

We make a portion of our mailing list available to reputable third parties that offer products we believe may interest you. If you prefer that we not exchange your name with third parties, or if you wish to clarify or modify your communication preferences, please visit us at www.ReaderService.com/consumerchoice or write to us at Harlequin Reader Service Preference Service, P.O. Box 9062, Buffalo, NY 14269. Include your complete name and address.

HILP13R